That's the Way, is a Vamp

and other Quintessentially Quirky Tales

Iain Pattison

First published in Great Britain in 2015 by DoubleQ Books
www.doubleqbooks.com

Guest story Growing Out of Burgers
© 2015 by Sally Jenkins
All other stories © 2015 by Iain Pattison

Cover illustration by Jean Hill
Formatting and design by Peter Jones
Editing by Maureen Vincent-Northam

All rights reserved

No part of this publication may be reproduced, stored in a retrieval system, or transmitted, in any form or by any means, without the prior permission in writing of the publisher. This is a work of the imagination. Names, characters, places and incidents are used fictitiously and any resemblance to any persons, businesses, locales or events is entirely coincidental.

Designed and produced in Great Britain by
DoubleQ Books

ISBN: 978-1533209412

British Cataloguing Publication data:
A catalogue record of this book is available from
the British Library

This book is also available as an ebook

About The Author

Humorist Iain Pattison has been entertaining readers on both sides of the Atlantic for 20 years with a succession of short stories that have won prize after prize, appeared in magazines and anthologies, and been broadcast on the UK's most prestigious speech radio station, BBC Radio 4.

As well as penning quirky tales, he is a creative writing tutor, competition judge and after dinner speaker.

Originally from Glasgow, he now lives in Birmingham – until the city council find a way of legally removing him…

To learn more about Iain follow him on twitter @AuthorIain or visit iainpattison.com

About Our Guest Story Author

Accomplished short story writer Sally Jenkins' work wows magazine readers and competition judges in equal measure. Her e-collections are a critical hit on Amazon and her articles about the writing life frequently appear in the UK writing press.

She likes to surprise readers with a final twist, turning everything that's gone before on its head, or to apply the emotional thumbscrews, pulling readers into the rollercoaster of her characters' lives. The Museum of Fractured Lives, a linked series of three longer stories, features both of these tactics.

When not busy at the keyboard, she enjoys Body Combat classes and church bell ringing.

Follow her blog at sally-jenkins.com

Contents

THAT'S WHY THE LADY IS A VAMP	1
NO TIME LIKE THE PRESENT	8
IN A RIGHT HUMP	22
GHOST IMAGE	24
PUBLISH AND BE DAMNED!	31
BRIEF ENCOUNTER	41
HUE AND CRY	52
VIRGIN TERRITORY	55
POET TREE IN MOH-SHAN	70
JUST IMAGINE	73
CS–AYE, JIMMY	79
CHEATER	87
CRAZY PAVING	90

A SOONFUL OF SPUGAR 96

GROWING OUT OF BURGERS 99

That's Why the Lady is a Vamp

Ivana snorted impatiently, snapping her fingers at the liveried flunky.

"C'mon man, get a move on. I haven't got all night."

Apologising profusely, the doorman bowed and held out his hand to help Ivana struggle from the back of the limousine. Her figure-hugging designer dress was so restrictive that it would have choked the life out of any normal mortal. But she was, she thought wryly, neither normal nor mortal.

She paused in mid manoeuvre to make sure the posse of waiting cameramen caught a teasing shot of her beautiful bare upper thigh before stepping onto the Manhattan sidewalk.

Turning her million-dollar smile on them, she revealed perfect, white, sharp supermodel's teeth. The smile didn't travel up to her eyes – not just because she felt little warmth or empathy but because she was desperately avoiding the painful explosions of brilliance. Damn the flashbulbs – they were as strong as daylight!

"Ivana! Ivana! Is there any truth in the rumours? Are you engaged? Has he proposed yet?" a voice yelled.

"Are you going to be wife number six?" another added.

Tapping the side of her nose mischievously, she turned from the reporters and the flood of questions. Let them wait, let them stew.

The press were parasites, and she hated them with a cold, burning loathing, but she also respected the fact that they were incredibly powerful and deadly to cross. Ruthless – just like herself. Merciless – just like all of her kindred. And just as determined when they scented blood.

Striding so fast that the sapphire necklace around her porcelain-pale throat bounced, she entered the towering glass and chrome corporate office block.

She was late for her assignation, but she doubted that Donald would notice. He'd be too busy on the phones turning his modest 3-billion fortune into a more respectable 4-billion fortune.

As the reception desk staff signed her in, she let her gaze rise to the various balconies and upper floors; to the stern-faced men in dark suits and crew cuts, men sporting crackling earpieces and high-velocity rifles. All of them watching her – watching like hawks – waiting for any sudden move, any excuse to open fire.

Let them dare, she thought with amusement. It was unlikely they'd bring her down with their first volley, and she'd rip out their windpipes before they had time to fire off a second. Even though the diamante encrusted four-inch heels might slow her up just a little...

She sighed. The overblown security was all so silly, so pointless, but since they'd started dating she'd learnt to put up with Donald's paranoia; ignoring the tiny crucifix around his neck, the strange aftershave that smelt vaguely of garlic and the new ultra-violet lighting system installed at both his luxury apartment and his office complex. Plus, the sudden arrival of all these ex-special forces bodyguards.

"Anyone would think you don't feel safe around me," she'd pouted at their last public appearance, a glitzy charity fundraiser for underprivileged families in her native Carpathian region.

"I do," he'd answered, with a dry chuckle, "but it never does any harm to have a little insurance. We wouldn't want any misunderstandings, any little playful accidents to spoil things, now would we?"

The private elevator dispatched from the penthouse level pinged open and, waving teasingly to the stony-faced assassins, she got in and pressed the button.

Goons and guns aside, it was a perfect relationship, she mused as the glass lift rose smoothly floor by floor. A super-rich sugar daddy passionate for Eastern European beauties with bodies to die for, and a woman who never got a day older – or wanted to hang around until morning.

So were the reporters right, she asked herself. Was tonight the night? Was he finally going to pop the question? Was it going to be 'til death us do part?

"Ivana, my darling, you look even more radiant than usual," Donald said, getting up from the long table and pushing back his unruly hair.

She brushed his mahogany-tanned cheek with her lips, giving him a tiny nip – a promise of things to come.

"You don't look so bad yourself," she purred. "For someone who has the constant headache of having to sack so many incompetent trainees."

He gestured her to sit, a momentary frown making his bushy brows dip. "I'm glad you could come over, because I've being doing some reflecting..." he began.

"Not something I can claim," she joked, tilting her head coquettishly.

"...and I think it's time to put our relationship on a more serious, more permanent basis."

She felt butterflies in her stomach – little crimson butterflies. At last!

"And I'd like to ask you if you'd make me the

happiest man in the world by consenting to… consenting to…"

Oh yes, oh yes!

"…meeting a business associate of mine."

Ivana did a double take, stunned. Her hearing was super sensitive, the stuff of legend, but she was sure her ears were playing tricks. Business associate? What business associate? Where was the proposal? The grand romantic gesture? The engagement ring sporting a diamond so big it could power a death ray?

"I think you may have heard of him," Donald said, pressing the desk buzzer, summoning a dark, funereal figure in wide-brimmed hat, cloak, gauntlets and riding boots. "He's from the Old Country."

She froze. Oh yes, she recognised him all right. Van Helsing! The nemesis of all of her kind.

"It's been a long time, Ivana," the newcomer said, voice measured, eyes locking fearlessly on hers.

"Arguably, not long enough," she hissed, hackles rising. Spinning round to Donald, she demanded: "Why have you brought him here? Is this a trap? Are you trying to destroy me? What's going on?"

The billionaire shrugged sheepishly. "You know I love you more than anyone else on the planet, and I desperately want you to be my wife. But with who you are – what you are – I need to take a few precautions."

Van Helsing stepped forward. "With your reputation, it is only common sense to have safeguards," he explained, dumping his large canvas travelling bag onto the boardroom table. "I have been called in to ensure you never bleed Donald dry."

He reached inside, and Ivana stiffened. Shivering with fear she watched, transfixed, as he brought out the only instrument in the entire universe that terrified her. Not Holy Water, silver bullets or a weapon personally blessed by the Pope, but something immensely more powerful, something guaranteed to stop her dead in her tracks.

"We both know you've seen one of these before," the newcomer observed slyly, his Transylvanian accent suddenly more pronounced.

She couldn't help herself – Ivana flinched, repelled more effectively than if it had been a cross.

Staring furiously at the ancient parchment, she knew the game was up. Curse him! Curse Van Helsing! Curse all those sworn to thwart her sinking her teeth into a fresh victim.

"I suppose this is what they mean by raising the stakes," she ventured ruefully as, defeated, she turned to leave. "Well, it's been a good run. I almost pulled it off. Until next time…"

"I'll be waiting," the divorce lawyer agreed amicably, and stuffed the unsigned pre-nup agreement back into his battered voluminous valise.

No Time Like the Present

The blast blew me half way across the office. Cart-wheeling through the air, I hit the filing cabinets hard and fell groaning to the floor as a blizzard of glass rained down on me.

Dazed and bleeding I crawled under my desk frantically seeking some sort of safety. My ears throbbed from the booming shock wave and the banshee scream of the security alarm.

What the hell had happened? I shook myself, trying to make my brain kick back into action. There'd been an explosion, but where? How?

My mobile rang and I snatched it from where it lay dented and battered in the rubble.

It was Frank Peters, my deputy. "It's the particle accelerator lab," he told me, voice tight with excitement and fear. "Most of the block is gone; levelled. The proton exciter is a pile of twisted scrap and the rest is burning wreckage. It's a bloody shambles, Jack."

My heart sank. There were nine scientists in there at any time, manning the silvery doughnut-shaped atom smasher.

"Any word on casualties?" I asked, dreading the answer. "How many are hurt?"

I could hear Frank swallow hard. "No-one got out alive," he said softly. "They're all dead. Everyone is dead."

I fought the urge to throw up.

"Okay," I told him. "Call a priority one alert. Until we know what's going on, I want the entire base evacuated. I'm on my way. Don't let anyone near the blast site until I get there."

Staggering outside, I headed for my car. Thoughts of sabotage attacks and sneak terrorist bombings flashed across my mind, but I knew our security was too good for that.

No, this had to be the terrible accident I'd been dreading since our boffins announced they were intending to recreate the conditions that existed at the very beginnings of the universe. For months they'd been colliding supercharged positrons and electrons at astonishing speeds.

"We're dying to learn what the Big Bang was like," they'd excitedly told the world's scientific community.

Well, it looked like they'd got their wish.

Frowning, I sped across the outer perimeter towards the main section of the base. I could imagine that night's news when journalists got word of the blast and the TV crews turned up. It was going to be a circus.

As head of security at The Institute I'd warned the base commander about the dangers of the experiments weeks earlier. The equipment was too powerful and unstable; too dangerous. But he hadn't listened.

"It's not a security matter," he'd said. "I appreciate your input, Jack, but I think we'll leave health and safety concerns to the experts, don't you? Doctor Cartwright and his team know what they're doing."

The fool. How wrong he'd been, how stupidly negligently wrong. With those scientists killed it had become a whooping great security matter.

I felt anger surge through me. Jerking the wheel over, I spun the car round the corner, up to the gatehouse at the entrance to the research wing. The soldiers on guard looked dazed, clutching their rifles with whitened knuckles.

I'd never really bothered to look at them before but it struck me just how young they seemed. They barely looked old enough to have enlisted, never mind be put guarding one of the country's most sensitive research establishments.

Another thought hit me as I drove through the huge chain-link gates. Hadn't the concrete guard bunker just been repainted? It had been sparkling white the last time I'd seen it. Now, it seemed dull and shabby – as though it hadn't seen a lick of paint in years.

It was odd, but I shrugged it off. It must be a result of the blast damage.

Frank was waiting for me, his car parked beside the convoy of fire engines and ambulances. He'd taken me at my word. No-one had been allowed anywhere near the devastated laboratories.

"You look like shit," he said, motioning to the cuts and bruises on my face.

"I've been better," I conceded.

"All non-essential personnel have been evacuated, as you requested and I've paged Doctor Mitchells," Frank said. "I thought we might need him. They're helicoptering him in."

I nodded. It was a smart move. Mitchells was one of The Institute's top scientists, a typical mad professor, but a good man to have around in a crisis.

"Are we absolutely sure that no-one's left alive?" I asked. There was no sense putting the emergency crews at risk unnecessarily.

"No chance of survivors," Frank replied bleakly. "No-one could have lived through the blast. It ripped the lab buildings clean off their foundations."

I glanced through the fence to where a quarter of an acre of flattened destruction smouldered sadly. It was impossible to believe that just minutes before this had been a complex of concrete, toughened glass and re-enforced steel. The place had been levelled as though a squadron of B52 bombers had used it for target practice.

The whacking noise of the base helicopter announced Doctor Mitchells' arrival. Ducking below the spinning rotors he came running over at a crouch.

"My God," he said, when he saw the scene. "It's unbelievable! I've never seen anything like it."

"Total destruction," I agreed. "The force must have been incredible. What would have caused an explosion that big?"

Mitchells frowned, grey eyebrows puckering. "They must have been running the accelerator at full pelt. It's a dangerous procedure at the best of times." He shrugged. "But if they reversed the polarity on the Celeron discharger at the same time…"

He mimed an explosion.

I turned to Frank.

"You look like shit," he said, motioning to the cuts and bruises on my face.

"I've been better," I conceded.

My stomach spasmed as I felt reality take a sideways step.

"Didn't you just say that to me?" I asked, hoping that it was just one of those silly moments of déjà vu.

"Did I say what?" Frank asked, puzzled, and looked up to the helicopter coming in to land nearby. Doctor Mitchells jumped out and was running towards us, crouched under the spinning rotor blades.

I did a double take. It wasn't possible. He was here already. I'd spoken to him. I spun to where he'd been standing just a second before. The space was empty!

"My God," he said as he surveyed the scene. "It's unbelievab–"

I cut across him. "Doc, something weird is going on here. I don't understand it but I think we've got big trouble."

* * *

I couldn't blame Doctor Mitchells for thinking I was losing my marbles. He had no memory of talking to me about Celeron dischargers and particle accelerators. As far as he was concerned he'd just arrived.

"There are two possibilities," he said, his face darkening. "You were more badly injured in the explosion than you think. You may have a bad concussion or–"

"Or?" I prompted anxiously.

"Or the explosion had somehow damaged the fabric of space and time."

I hoped it was the first option. A bump on the head I could cope with. Having the universe doing crazy things was too scary to contemplate.

I thought about the way the guard-house bunker had reverted to its pre-decoration drabness and a chill ran through me.

"It seems that time is hiccupping backwards and forwards," Mitchells observed when I told him about the suspiciously young guards.

His face suddenly filled with fear. "Use the rocket launcher," he screamed. "It's our only hope!"

What? I looked at him as though he was mad. What rocket launcher? What was he babbling on about?

"There are two possibilities," he remarked, face darkening. "You were more badly injured in the explosion than you th–"

I grabbed him. "Doc," I yelled. "We're stuck in some sort of time loop. We need to get away from here."

Dragging him away, I glanced over my shoulder. Where the labs had been was now a green field with a sign announcing the planned construction of a complex of research buildings. The completion date said: October 1996!

* * *

"You look like shit," Frank told me, motioning to the cuts and bruises on my face.

I ignored him, concentrating on getting us all away from the blast site. If we could just get into the car and off the base's research wing we might be able to warn the authorities. I didn't know what they'd be able to do about a time rift, but that was their problem.

I almost wept as I stared at my car. The gleaming new Lexus was gone. In its place stood a model–T Ford!

"It appears the effects are gaining momentum," Doc Mitchells said, half to himself. "This is serious. If it's not stopped there's no telling what will happen. Time could collapse in on itself."

Closing my eyes I cursed those egghead idiots who'd thought they could just muck about with malevolently charged sub-atomic molecules. God knows what catastrophe they'd set in motion.

Roughly bundling Frank and the Doc on to the model–T, I cranked it up and we were off towards the gatehouse. The bunker shell was flickering like a mirage: old and shabby, then dazzling white. As we sped past I could see the guards. In one instant they were toddlers crawling around the ground, the next grey-haired, wizened old men!

I was too busy staring at them to see the horse blocking the road. I hit the brakes and swung the wheel over hard. We skidded to a halt, half in a ditch. The gun was an antique, but it looked deadly enough.

"Stand fast and deliver," the highwayman shouted.

He fired and a small metal ball imbedded in the dashboard as Doc Mitchells said: "It seems that time is hiccupping backwards and forwards–"

The masked figure went for a second musket – and pointed it straight at my head. I yelled just as reality shifted sideways again and we found ourselves standing back at the explosion site. I looked down at my watch. The hands were spinning backwards.

This was getting too damn crazy! Frank's face drained of all colour. "What the hell is that?" he shouted, pointing. I followed the line of his arm and realised our troubles were just beginning.

* * *

It danced madly across the blast site, bobbing up and down like a kid's balloon. It was difficult at first to tell what it was, but as it came nearer I could see that it was some sort of tornado; a spinning, churning, roaring vortex.

It was sucking in matter, objects twisting and elongating as they streamed into it. Everything in its path was being stretched and devoured, whisked away to God knows where.

"It's an inter-dimensional rip in the fabric of space," Mitchells whispered, awed. "The explosion must have caused a breach. It's distorting time, tearing the continuum apart."

I didn't know what he meant but I knew it was bad, as bad as it gets.

"Can we stop it?" I asked, unable to take my eyes off the screaming hateful whirlpool that was tugging and chewing at reality.

"I don't know," he replied. "This is beyond my expertise. This is unknown outside of the wildest speculations of theoretical quantum physics. Your guess is as good as mine."

I grimaced. So much for science.

Frank grabbed my arm. "Look," he said excitedly. "An explosion caused this thing. Maybe another explosion can stop it."

"Yes!" Mitchells agreed. "It's possible. The force of a second blast might seal the rift."

I did some quick thinking. The Institute was MoD-funded so there were all sorts of explosives on site – but what to use, and how much?

The vortex lurched towards us, sucking down a length of metal fencing in one noisy gulp.

Then I remembered the Doc's earlier outburst. He'd yelled about using a rocket launcher. It hadn't meant anything then but now it made all the sense in the world.

It took ten minutes to locate the hefty weapon in the arms store and break it out of its secured housing. By the time I'd sprinted back with it, the vortex was twice as big, the air around it crackling with electricity as cars flew through the air and disappeared into its ravenous jaws.

I looked pleadingly into Doc Mitchells' eyes.

"Are you sure this is going to work?" I asked softly.

"No," he admitted, "but it's the only option we've got."

He warned that the missile must explode just as it entered the lip of the tornado. If it worked, we'd shut the inter-dimensional door. There was no margin for error and no chance for a practice shot.

"Ah well, no time to lose," I muttered sardonically and shoved the rocket into the firing tube.

The vortex was a moving target and, as I struggled to get a lock on it, I asked myself questions I couldn't answer. What if I failed, would the rift grow larger and larger until it swallowed up everything on the planet?

I lost concentration for an instant because the next thing I knew it was upon us. I felt my body being pulled, sucked, twisted.

The Doc's face suddenly filled with fear. "Use the rocket launcher," he screamed. "It's our only hope!"

I didn't need telling a third time. I took aim at the screeching circle of destruction, gulped and fired. The excruciating roar seemed loud enough to shatter my eardrums. It felt like someone was trying to scoop out my brains with a spoon.

The shock wave hit us a millisecond later, lifting us clear off the ground and sending us sprawling. We landed painfully on the concrete several feet away, giving me a whole new set of bruises to add to my growing collection.

"Look," Frank yelled, pointing towards the vortex. "Something's happening. It's changing."

He was right. As we gazed in amazement, the whirlpool shuddered and slowed its spin. It was rotating at only a fraction of its speed – and it was shrinking!

"The second blast is pulling the ripped edges together," Doc Mitchells hissed over the noise. "It's working!"

I sighed in relief, but I knew we weren't in the clear yet. The vortex was still remorselessly sucking in objects, still distorting the space and time around it. Things could still go terribly wrong...

The whirlpool grew smaller and smaller, the furious bellowing roar diminishing rapidly.

"Keep going," Frank urged it, fist clenched. "Just a little bit more."

A tree flew over our heads towards the spinning circle, then suddenly dropped like a boulder as the vortex snapped shut.

I don't know which frightened me more – the giant oak crashing to the ground just inches away, or the sight of the vortex folding in on itself and disappearing with an electric whip-crack.

"We've done it," Mitchells yelped, jumping up and down. "We've closed the fissure."

I was about to smile, but something wiped it from my face.

"Good Lord," I gasped as I looked across at the devastation that had been the physics labs. Something was happening – something really weird!

Chunks of wreckage were leaping off the ground and sticking together, as they went in a blink of an eye from blackened debris to colourful painted fragments of wood. Whole sections of building were magically gluing together like an invisible giant's construction set.

All around the site, fiery rubble transformed itself as tongues of flame unlicked the damaged framework of the buildings. Glass shards flew at high speed, a snowstorm of tiny pieces colliding and coalescing into whole unblemished sheets.

Time was running backwards! The explosion was un-doing itself, repairing the damage!

"I don't believe this," I muttered, shaking my head. "It just isn't possible."

Over at the guard-house bunker, the concrete shell was growing whiter by the instant, as though an unseen giant had picked up a brush and begun slapping on paint.

"Time is reverting to its pre-blast state," Mitchells told me, his voice now low in awe. "It'll be as though the explosion never happened."

This was madness, but I was ecstatic. If there had been no accident then the scientists weren't dead! No-one had been harmed!

I hugged myself with glee as time sprung back to its previous course. It was like watching a film winding backwards, the labs reassembling in a mesmerising aerial ballet.

"I don't know what we're going to tell people," I observed. "No-one's going to believe us." I pointed down at the stolen missile launcher. "And I think I might have some awkward explaining to do."

Mitchells patted me reassuringly on my arm. "It'll be okay," he promised. "I'll tell them that you were sealing up a rip in the fabric of the universe."

Frank grinned. "Yeah, don't worry, Jack. We'll explain it was an emergency sewing job – a stitch in time that saved nine!"

In a Right Hump

Cursing and kicking the Cathedral cat, Quasimodo trooped dispiritedly down the 387 steps from the tower. It had been a pig of a day and he couldn't wait to clock off.

Friends told him he should be thrilled to be working at Notre Dame and being its top attraction. But he was sick of the tourists and their stupid questions, sick of signing autographs and most definitely sick of posing with them for sketches. God, he hated it!!!!

Limping along the dark Paris street, he thought about jacking it all in. Okay, he was misshapen and stooped – with a face that curdled milk – but this was 1482 and anything was possible for a man with a few good ideas, an engaging lisp and an entrepreneurial flair.

Perhaps, today – this most awful of days – was the time to finally take the plunge and start that beautician's business.

But first, he needed a drink.

Although the tavern was crowded he spotted a free space at the bar. At the fifth attempt he made it up on to the stool.

"You look awful," Pierre the bar-keep said, deadpan. "Bad day?"

"Like you wouldn't believe," Quasi grumbled. "A baying mob turned up this afternoon with pitchforks and flaming torches. They called me a monster; wanted to hang me by the gargoyles."

"Painful," Pierre observed sympathetically. "But why would they want to kill you? I thought you were the big star, a real draw."

"I am, but according to them it's..." The seething campanologist made quotation marks in the air. "...traditional at this time of year to lynch deformed dwarves."

Both men agreed it wasn't very politically correct, but could understand the argument for protecting the nation's customs and heritage.

"Still," Pierre consoled, "you've always got the love of a good woman. Your Esmeralda is a diamond."

"She left me," Quasi said sadly. "Packed her bags and went to her mother's. Said my constant moaning put her back up."

Yes, Pierre agreed with an expressive Gallic shrug, that romantic blow alone would be enough to make anyone bitter and twisted. There was nothing else for it. Only a stiff drink would do.

Reaching for the Johnnie Walker bottle the barman went to pour a dram, but Quasimodo waved his hand frantically at the whisky next to it – his favourite brand.

"The Bell's, the Bell's," he insisted.

Ghost Image

"I'm telling you, the variances are nearly off the scale." Naomi's voice betrayed her rising excitement. "I've got a 12 point 6 reading. This place is crawling with psychic energy. It's alive with it!"

Frowning, Justin looked up from the control desk. "You must have the instruments set wrongly. A reading that high is impossible."

Naomi glared at him, a tell-tale pulse fluttering at her temple. "Impossible or not. I'm telling you that I'm getting multiple spectre readings. This dump isn't just haunted, it's running a spook convention."

Justin sighed. This was all he needed. It was Naomi's first outing with the group and he'd half expected her to freak out. She was that type – nervy, highly strung. He cursed Alan. He should never have let his research partner twist his arm into bringing the girl along.

As leader of the college's paranormal research team, Justin was against novices on field trips. They got wound up, edgy and clumsy. They invariably fouled up things and got under everyone's feet.

But Alan had been insistent.

"She's a good kid," he'd said, "bright, keen, intuitive. She'll be a real asset to the team. She's very willing."

Justin had smiled dryly at that. I'll bet she's very willing, he'd thought. But he owed the senior tutor a favour, so nineteen-year-old student Naomi had joined him, Alan and technician Zac in giving Parklands Grange the once over.

As stately homes went, Parklands was very far down the grandeur scale. Large parts had fallen into disrepair, while the remainder of the building had a fading, shabby elegance. As haunted houses went it was a minor league location – barely worth a second look. It boasted the occasional temperature anomaly, creaking floorboard and groaning from the attic, but nothing that would make the front page of Psychic News. No headless horsemen, floating nuns or demon hounds.

That's why it was left to a small-time operation like Justin's to go poking around there. And that's why Naomi's reading was so obviously wrong.

Frown deepening, Justin looked over to the corner of the main hall where Zac was setting up temperature sensors. The technician shrugged back.

"Perhaps she's getting a ghost image," Zac suggested, pushing his lank hair out of his eyes.

He groaned when he realised what he'd said. "Sorry. No pun intended. I was just thinking that most of the tech is held together with gaffer tape and solder. It wouldn't surprise me if half this junk was giving off false readings."

Justin's eyes flicked over to Alan. "Well, is it possible?"

His fellow tutor shook his head. "No way. The kit is correctly calibrated. I checked it myself this evening before we set out."

Alan walked over to Naomi and looked over her shoulder. "She's right. It reads 12 point 6."

Naomi gave Justin a triumphant 'I-told-you-so' smirk but he didn't register it. His mind raced. A reading that high could only mean multiple phantoms – several ghosts haunting at once. He slowly licked his lips. This could be big, really big. A break like this could make him.

"Okay," he told the others, "we're going to give this one the works. I want constant VT filming; heat sensors, a link-up between the motion detectors and the stills cameras; a constant sweep of the outer rooms for electrical static build-up, and microphones everywhere. If a mouse as much as sneezes, I want it on digital recorder."

The team worked quickly, connecting the long snakes of wiring to the computer-controlled panel. As Zac angled infra red lights to illuminate the passageways, Justin tested the mikes. He could hear everything – even Naomi's muffled giggle as Alan stretched across her to plug in the VT playback monitor.

Justin felt momentary annoyance, but pushed it away. He'd have it out with Alan later. Meantime, he needed to keep his full attention on the tests. Eventually the hardware was all in place and working. If there was the slightest psychic activity, they'd capture it.

"What happens now?" Naomi asked, as they settled down on the hall floor with sandwiches and coffee flasks.

"We wait," Justin told her. As they looked nervously around the room, his watch alarm beeped. It was midnight.

* * *

Justin woke with a start. His first thought was: it's beginning! But as he glanced over at the control panel, he could see the equipment idling, still on stand-by.

He nudged Zac awake and they both checked the read-outs. Apart from the earlier reading, it was all quiet. As quiet as the grave, Justin told himself. He looked questioningly at the technician.

"No change," Zac said, stifling a yawn. "Temperature's down a bit on normal, but that might just be draughts in a big old place like this. No obvious cold spots."

Justin looked down at the other two. Alan was asleep, his arm around Naomi's waist. The girl was nuzzled up to the tutor's balding head.

Fighting the urge to kick them, Justin looked at his watch. It read 4.46am. He knew it would be dawn in a few moments, and that would be an end to it. There wouldn't be any ghosts appearing once daylight came streaming through the windows.

Justin felt awful. The thermos was empty and he had a crick in his neck from the cold floor. The first rays of morning pierced the gloom.

"Okay, that's it. We're packing up." He clapped his hands loudly. Moaning in protest, Alan and Naomi got uneasily to their feet.

"What's going on?" Alan asked, rubbing his eyes.

"Nothing, absolutely nothing. That's why I'm pulling the plug. This is a total waste of time." Justin gave the girl a withering glance. "Twelve point six on the scale? I'll bet. It's been a real amateur fun night, hasn't it?"

Naomi stiffened angrily.

"What do you mean by that?" Alan demanded, putting his arm around her.

"Just that if you spent more time hunting ghosts and less time hunting bits of skirt, then maybe we might get somewhere. This has been a complete fiasco." Justin shook his head irritably. "Zac and I will put the stuff in the van. Join us when you two lovebirds are ready."

* * *

Ten minutes later, the van pulled off down the long driveway. Concentrating on his driving, Justin ignored the frosty atmosphere. He didn't care. He was sick of Alan's amorous antics.

In the back, Naomi sniffled into a paper hankie. "The reading was right," she whined. "It's not my fault nothing happened. I wanted to see ghosts more than any of you."

Shrugging, Justin snapped: "And you might have, if Alan had checked out our equipment as much as he checked out yours."

He expected Alan to respond angrily, but wasn't prepared for the fist that cannoned into the side of his face. He swung round, half stunned and the SUV lurched over to the right, skidding madly on the gravel.

Justin barely had time to see the tree before they hit it. The force of the impact caved in the front of the van. Justin and Zac were killed outright. Alan and the girl were only knocked unconscious, but it made no difference. They perished as the ruptured petrol tank caught light with a roar, engulfing the vehicle.

A wall of flame lapped hungrily at the mangled wreckage, but as it did so the SUV seemed to grow dim. Moment by moment, its image waned and faded. Within minutes it had gone... melted away.

* * *

"I'm telling you, the variances are nearly off the scale," Naomi's voice betrayed her rising excitement. "I've got a 12 point 6 reading. This place is crawling with psychic energy."

Justin frowned. She must have got it wrong. Parklands Grange was a third division haunting site. A reading that high was impossible.

He began to argue with her when he suddenly sensed they'd had the quarrel before.

For a moment he felt his sense of reality shudder, then the sensation was gone. Justin didn't give it a second thought – he had more important things to worry about.

A reading that high could only mean multiple spectres – several ghosts haunting at once.

He did a quick mental calculation. He couldn't be totally certain but he reckoned they were looking for four phantoms...

Publish and be Damned!

A sudden commotion made Geraint jump; the hand scripted galley proofs he'd been scrutinising tumbling chaotically to the printing house floor. Outside, in the busy cobbled street, he could hear the air fill with shouts of anger and protest.

Bustling over to the mullioned window, the publisher took in the scene and immediately cursed.

It couldn't be! Not again! But yes, he realised wearily, the ecclesiastical whirlwind was returning.

Scything through the crowd, swinging his sharp-edged crook from side to side, Bishop John Henry was making a beeline towards Geraint's premises. Face crimson, voice tight and thunderous, he bellowed with every swipe: "Let me through. Let me through, I say. I am on the Lord's holy mission and I shall not be delayed for an instant. Stand aside."

Around him, like baby chicks clinging to their demented mother, several clerics flustered and fretted, shooing away those annoyed bystanders who'd taken umbrage and severe damage to their shins.

Geraint's spirits sank like a witch on a ducking stool. Placing his palms tightly together, he prayed that the pissed-off prelate was going to veer off at the last moment and let his biblical wrath fall upon some other unfortunate business owner. But the boom of the mighty stave bouncing off the front door put paid to any hopes in that direction.

"Master Geraint. I demand you open up immediately," the Bishop roared, with all the bluster and ferocity he normally reserved for his fire and brimstone sermons.

Fumbling with the handle, Geraint racked his memory to identify what cardinal sin he could have committed. Could it be the sign in the window sparking this old testament tempest?

Since gaining the exclusive rights to print and sell bibles across the city, the bookbinder had hung up a notice saying: 'We take Holy Orders'. It had raised a few eyebrows, certainly, but surely the witticism hadn't been bad enough to warrant this? If it was, he calculated, the follow-up – 'We're devoted to our customers' – definitely wasn't going to see the light of day!

"At last," John Henry snarled, as the door flung open and he marched inside, dragging the vexed vergers behind him. "At last we can gain admittance to this den of vice and blasphemy, and put an end to the assault on the morals of the God-fearing public."

Den of vice? Assault on the morals of the public? Had the priest been at the communion wine? Or had wearing that heavy pointy hat finally crushed his brain? Geraint feared it was both.

"You are always most welcome inside my unworthy establishment, your Holiness," he began, with an obsequious bow. "You honour us with your most saintly presence. What may I help you with today?"

The churchman gave him a withering look, signalling that at this instant he'd give anything to be a canon with a cannon.

"Enough with the flannel, master printer. Enough of the grovelling, humble shopkeeper routine. It won't wash this time. You are in the most terrible trouble and you know why."

Geraint really didn't. He shrugged helplessly. "If it's about the mixed-up pen portraits in the last edition of the I Spy Directory of Clergymen, I've already apologised about that," he reminded.

"Not much of an apology as I recall," his visitor snapped back. "You seemed to think it amusing to tell me that you'd simply got your vicars in a twist!"

The peeved parson breathed in heavily. "No, what has brought me here today is immeasurably worse. An insult of biblical proportions. Nothing less than the work of Satan himself!"

He plunged his hand inside his robes and brought out a thick leather-bound volume, throwing it down on the nearby table with an echoing crash.

"This FILTH, this PORNOGRAPHY is an abomination, the most depraved obscenity my eyes have ever had the misfortune to behold!"

His cheeks puffed, rage turning his complexion rouge. "It is a vile, corrupting, lustful, scandalous publication designed to tempt even the most righteous and holy towards base and impure thoughts."

Geraint blinked. Half of his brain was thinking; Wow! Now that's what I call a Five-Star review while the other half was puzzling over how he'd somehow managed to overlook producing a sizzling, salacious, guaranteed best-seller sensation.

"But it's just a history book," he said in puzzlement, as he craned over to read the title of the offending tome. "Third Instalment of our Ancient Classics Chronicles. It's innocuous. Completely innocent."

Around them the ring of anxious acolytes swallowed hard, crossed themselves and edged back a step from the inevitable explosion.

"There is nothing innocent in this Devil's digest," John Henry roared. "It is perversion in its rawest form. And I mean – raw!"

With that, the pontiff flipped open the book.

Geraint couldn't help himself. He'd uttered: "Holy Moly!" before he could prevent the stunned words spilling out.

If anything the angry cleric had understated the lewdness of the offending volume's contents. The sight that greeted the publisher's bulging eyes was unbelievable. Every drawing, every sketch, every image was unadulterated erotic titillation.

Page after page of bawdiness greeted him. Acres of bare skin, rude romps and carefree copulation adorned the parchment; each illumination shining a licentious light on activities that should definitely be kept in the dark!

"But I never authorised this," he gasped, as he studied the scenes of floosies and sandalled fighting men engaged in manhandling manoeuvres, and shuddered at the accompanying sex-filled storyline. "I simply told the author to make the Grecian era a bit more stimulating."

In that, the Bishop observed icily, the scribe had most certainly met his brief. "Who committed this foul act? Who is responsible?" he demanded.

Geraint sighed. "That will be Old Vic," he replied glumly. "All our histories are written by the Victor."

Closing the salacious hardback with a snap, jolting several of the gawping Reverends out of their reverie, John Henry raised himself to his full height and instructed: "Then take me to him at once."

"You intend to communicate?" Geraint ventured.

"I intend to ex-communicate," the Bishop corrected menacingly.

* * *

They made their way in procession up the rickety wooden steps and along a dusty corridor until Geraint halted them before a door bearing the copperplate notice: *Vic's Heritage History Books — always busy making royalties from Royalty!*

None of the party smiled.

"Perhaps, I should go in first," the publisher suggested. "Just to have a quiet word with Victor, to get his side of the story. I'm sure there's a perfectly reasonable explanation for all this."

But John Henry wasn't having any of it.

"Stand aside," he commanded, pushing forward roughly. "I haven't time for your mealy-mouthed chats. I want an interrogation, a probing investigation. I want to get to the bottom of this outrage."

And letting a malicious growl enter his voice, added: "Indeed, when I get my hands and red hot poker on this heinous heretic, I intend to perform an outrage on his bottom."

Victor blinked in surprise as they spilled into his cramped writing room. He obviously wasn't expecting visitors, never mind an inquisition – Spanish or otherwise.

"W-w-what's the meaning of this," he gasped, as he navigated his way out from behind walls of precariously piled papers, mildewed maps and wilted wills.

The Bishop's eyes narrowed. "No, that's my question, scurrilous scribe. What's the meaning of..." He jabbed his ring adorned finger at one of the offending pictures. "...this!"

Victor flipped his spectacles from high on his forehead on to the bridge of his bony nose, and focused intently on the indicated coloured plate in the crisis-causing Chronicle.

"Ah, that's the fall of Troy," he reported, with a scholarly sniff. "The moment when the Athenian call girls seduced the guards, distracting them so that the city gates could be opened, allowing the invaders to pour in."

For a second Geraint thought the Bishop was going to faint. For that matter, the printer thought he might have a swoon himself. What was this rubbish?

"Call girls?" John Henry said, choking. "Athenian call girls!"

Victor nodded, beaming innocently.

"Seduced the guards?" the prelate repeated, aghast.

"Oh yes," the author agreed happily. "It was the turning point in the ten-year-old siege, when the courtesans were left on the beach. Agamemnon knew the Trojan soldiers wouldn't be able to resist the allure of these ladies of the night. One glimpse of their voluptuous bodies and the troops would instantly forget the old adage: beware the gift of bare Greeks."

Geraint didn't know whether to laugh or cry. To be on the safe side, he did a little of both.

"I have never heard such a blatant distortion of the facts in all my life," the stunned Bishop declared, as he shook his head and crook in perfect synchronisation. "This is some fantastical fiction; a fabrication. There was no fornication mentioned in Homer's Iliad, no hussies recorded in any other historical account. How, in God's name, did you get the idea that this ancient war was ended by women of easy virtue. Who told you this nonsense?"

Victor pointed straight at his employer. "He did."

Geraint spluttered, mouth falling open.
What!

"N-n-o, I didn't," he contradicted loudly. "That's a lie. I did nothing of the sort." He held up both hands to show how vehemently he denied the very suggestion.

"Yes, you did. You specifically told me to include the jezebels." Victor turned to address the apoplectic apostle, revealing conspiratorially: "I remember it clearly, your Worshipfulness. He was very insistent. He wanted as many pictures as I could sketch. Every detail, he said, include every detail. Make it exciting... so I did."

Geraint gulped. The publisher didn't know what lunacy was at work here, but he reckoned it could only end in one way – with him being invited to the Bishop's very unique poker game, where no amount of bluffing would be enough to save his rump from a roasting.

"I honestly have no idea what the senile old fool is raving on about," he protested desperately, looking round for a means of escape. "His brains must be addled. I never – repeat never – instructed him to include doxies in his drawings. I haven't a clue where he got that crazy notion from."

None of the churchmen appeared convinced. All glared accusingly at him, no doubt darkly imagining how satisfyingly the publisher's posterior would present as burnt offerings.

Then, suddenly, like a bolt from the very heavens, the answer struck him. Of course. It had to be!

Geraint groaned and covered his eyes as the hilarious solution to the rude riddle made itself blindingly clear.

And, grabbing the history scribe and pulling him close, the printer bellowed down Victor's trusty ear trumpet with enough force to send the cassocked assembly reeling.

"I was talking about a pony, you deaf sod. I didn't say whores – I said HORSE. Show lots of action of the guards celebrating with the Trojan Horse!"

Brief Encounter

Adam held his breath – his whole body taut.

"Have you reached a verdict on which you are all agreed?" the clerk of the court asked, voice booming across the dusty, old, walnut benches.

The jury forewoman nodded. "We have, your Honour."

"And to the charge that the accused stole goods to the value of £33,850? Do you find him guilty or not guilty?"

Adam closed his eyes, suddenly unable to watch. Was the middle-aged woman in the floral dress about to utter the words that would destroy his future?

"We find the defendant…"

Adam gulped.

"…Not Guilty."

Adam couldn't believe it. He let out his breath in a long relieved whoosh. He'd done it! He'd won! No conviction. No prison sentence.

"Congratulations," a female voice whispered in his ear. "You pulled it off. Nice going, Mr Phillips. We'll make a barrister of you yet."

Forcing open his eyes, Adam stared straight into the beautiful face of Penny Wilcott, QC – his opponent in the five–day legal battle – and mumbled thanks.

"I thought he'd be convicted for sure," he admitted, "the chap's alibi had more holes in it than a belly dancer's costume."

"I thought so too," Penny replied dryly. "Still, there's no accounting for the whims of juries. I'll chalk this one up to experience – although, Mr Phillips, you probably need the experience more than I do."

Adam, who'd only been in chambers just over a year, flushed at the mention of his relative newness. As a junior barrister, this was only his seventh case. It was also, he blushed to think, only his second win.

He bristled, ready to ward off the sarcastic attack he knew was coming but, to his surprise, Penny Wilcott smiled – a sudden warmth spreading across her stern prosecutor's features.

"I'm only teasing. I meant what I said. You did well. I'm impressed."

Glancing at her watch, she added. "It's too late to bother going back to chambers. How about a drink?"

Too surprised to answer, Adam blinked then nodded – the movement a bit too quick.

"Well... yes... I suppose... if you really want to. That's if you're not—"

She silenced him with one finger. "I insist. I'll buy. You've earned it and I always believe in encouraging rookies."

A mischievous gleam returned to her eye. "But don't you think you should congratulate your client first. He was expecting a two-year stretch – not a miracle acquittal. He's looking more shocked than you are."

* * *

The Wig and Pen was less than half full but the knot of noisy journalists at the bar made the pub seem busier.

"Sorry it took so long," Penny said as she came over with the drinks, "but I was listening to the reporters. They were discussing the verdict."

Adam's expression darkened. "Oh yes? What were they saying?"

"That you deserve a medal for getting Bobby Slater off," she replied, taking a long sip from her white wine. "It seems your summing-up speech had them blubbering. Not a dry eye in the house."

Glass halfway to his lips, Adam studied his companion's features for a clue. Was she pulling his leg? She had an infuriating way of digging fun while maintaining a deadpan expression.

In the three times they'd met, Penny Wilcott had angered and fascinated him in equal measure. Adam had never worked out if he hated her intensely or found her self-assured smugness alluring.

When he'd been given the Slater case, he'd been delighted to show what he could do. However, the joy had swiftly evaporated when he'd learnt who he'd be up against.

Ms Wilcott – one Penny definitely not from Heaven – was a fighter and a winner, and the notorious scourge of junior counsel.

"Here's to your victory," she said, tilting her glass in mock salute. "May it be the first of many... except when I'm up against you."

"You sound peeved," Adam replied, sipping his own drink. "Not used to losing?"

"Not to apprentices," she admitted. "Still, beginner's luck and all that. I'll get my revenge next time we face each other. I won't be so..."

She paused, seemingly searching for the right words.

"...taken in by a handsome face."

Adam spluttered in his wine. She was doing it again! Damn the woman! He'd never been any good at flirting and he squirmed at the thought that she might be leading him on just to slap him down with an acerbic one-liner.

"Well," he began, knowing that he was falling into a trap, "if I'm so handsome, I should be impossible to turn down... if I asked you to dinner, for instance."

She cocked her head to one side, challengingly. "If you asked me out to dinner? It's hypothetical, is it? Or are you actually asking me out?"

"Um… yes… I suppose." Adam cleared his throat. "Yes I am," he said more definitely. "We could go out one night next week, if you're free."

She shook her head.

"You're not free?"

"Oh, I'm free but I just don't think it would be such a good idea, do you? People might talk and I'd hate to be accused of cradle snatching."

Adam was about to spit out a reply, but Penny was already standing up, putting on her coat.

"Thanks anyway," she said, kissing him on the cheek. "It was a nice thought. Really sweet. Maybe one day, when you've joined the big boys."

With that she left. Burning with resentment, Adam watched her go. At that moment, he hated her more than any woman he'd ever known – yet knew he was hooked… hopelessly hooked.

* * *

Really sweet! When you've joined the big boys! How dare she! The memory of her put-downs stung bitterly for days.

Every spare moment Adam thought about her mysterious green eyes and the way her auburn hair bobbed when she shook her head. He couldn't shift the image of Penny's ready smile and the way her face changed – softening when she let down her guard for the most fleeting of seconds.

Then he'd remember her sardonic manner and defiant laugh and his nerves twisted.

Cradle snatching! He didn't know how old she was but it couldn't be much more than his 32 years. True, he'd been late coming into the profession – after a false start as a teacher – but he was no youngster. She may be a mighty Queen's Counsel but one day he'd take silk and then he'd show her.

He didn't know what made him do it – anger perhaps, or the sudden lure of the chase – but he found himself dialling the number of her chambers.

"Before you go on about me being a beginner and too junior to bother with, I want you to listen," he said, feeling rare courage. "I'm as good as you, as good as anyone, and I'll prove it. I'm up against you in a fraud next week and I promise I'll beat you. And it won't just be luck."

He pressed on, aware how silly he was sounding. "I'm laying down a challenge, a bet if you like. If you win I'll buy you a crate of champagne but if I win you take me out to dinner – somewhere very public – and you cut out all this cradle snatching rubbish."

He stopped, bravery ebbing. He tensed, waiting for Penny to pour scorn on his foolishness. Instead, she laughed – a strangely soft, musical laugh.

"About time too, my young friend. I wondered when you'd call. I was beginning to think you were a quitter. What a delightful idea. How could I refuse? Okay, I accept your challenge. However, I have to warn you that you stand no chance. Your client is as guilty as they come."

She laughed again, captivating him. "And I'm going to try extra hard this time. I love champagne – especially when someone else is paying for it."

* * *

Adam's eyes ached as he looked again at the defendant in the witness box. Every word Simmons said made him sound even more like the smooth career criminal he so obviously was.

"So you had no idea when you took these deposits for the land that you didn't, in fact, own it and thus couldn't legally sell it?" Penny Wilcott asked, voice heavy with irony.

"Good Lord, no," Simmons replied, with just enough exaggerated outrage to convince every member of the jury that this was a character who'd happily pinch the gold from a pensioner's teeth. "I was as shocked as anyone when I found out about the... misunderstanding."

Adam groaned inwardly. Penny Wilcott was right. Simmons was a shark and nothing was going to keep him out of jail.

For the last seven days Adam had scoured the case papers desperately looking for something to cast doubt on his client's guilt. Yet the more he read the police statements, the more hopeless it looked.

Adam kicked himself for rushing into the rash bet. It was a foregone conclusion. He was going to have to buy his grinning opponent the case of champagne and listen to her gloating.

He frowned. Maybe he WAS an innocent who needed protecting from himself. Maybe he WAS out of his league – professionally and romantically.

He looked across at Penny Wilcott who'd just finished questioning Simmons and who was now busy scribbling on a piece of paper.

"Do you have any further questions for your client, Mr Phillips?" the judge asked. "Do you wish to re-examine?"

Sighing, Adam nodded. It wouldn't do any good, of course, but he had to go through the motions.

As he rose to his feet, Penny leant across and passed the note.

It said: Make sure it's Bollinger. I don't want any old cheap rubbish.

* * *

"Three years isn't so bad," he told his client's family in the court building foyer. "It could have been worse. With good behaviour and remission he could be out in eighteen months or so."

Mrs Simmons wasn't having any of it. "What a right bloody waste of oxygen you turned out to be," she snarled. "I told Harry to get a proper brief but he wouldn't listen. Well, look where it's got him."

Depressed, Adam watched the family storm out. He knew there was a stinging truth in her angry words. Penny Wilcott would have got the man off, guilty or not. Anyone would – anyone but him.

"Cheer up," the familiar voice told him. "If it's any consolation I think you did the best anyone could. It was an impossible case right from the start."

Lifting his eyes wearily, Adam searched Penny's face for signs she was teasing. He didn't see any.

"I suppose you want your champagne now?"

"Absolutely. I'm looking forward to opening that first bottle tonight and tasting victory. Wonderful."

"I'll sort it out as soon as I get back to the office," he promised grumpily.

Watching her walk away with a jaunty step, he knew he should hate her – but all he could think of was how good she looked in black.

* * *

The email alert beeped just as a shocked Adam finished spending a week's fees on the wine merchant's website.

The short message started off with the address of a fashionable apartment block.

Max, the chambers clerk, looked at Adam as though he were mad.

"Pardon me saying this but you look as though you want to do a jig," Max observed, baffled. "I'd expected you to be devastated. I thought you lost."

Adam stared at the words on the screen: Bring the bubbly round at eight... with two glasses. I'll help you commiserate.

"No, Max, no," he replied, grinning broadly. "Whatever gave you that impression?"

Taking in the message's last line – And don't forget your toothbrush – Adam added, with a wink: "I have it on very good authority that, as of this moment, I'm definitely appealing!"

Hue and Cry

Snarling, Doctor Watson stormed out of the offices of *The Strand Magazine*, derisive laughter echoing in his ears.

It was outrageous. How dare the man, he fumed; fighting the urge to return and punch the smirking editor's nose.

The journalist's words stung like angry bees. "You've had a good run, Doc, but we'd look stupid publishing any more of your chronicles. This bizarre new direction Sherlock's taken doesn't exactly grip the punters."

Thrusting the barely read pages back into Watson's hands, he'd mocked: "These accounts are too dull for us. Why don't you try them elsewhere… like Homes and Gardens!"

During the Hansom ride back to Baker Street, Watson harboured thoughts that would have broken his Hippocratic Oath, if not his knuckles. But as the cab eventually pulled up outside 221b, he calmed, realising wearily that the magazine owner was right.

Since taking up his strange new hobby six months earlier, Holmes had lost interest in solving the baffling, glamorous, high-profile crimes that had made his name. And although the eccentric genius was still frantically busy, his forensic eye more tested and probing than ever, Sherlock's exploits could now only in one sense, be described as colourful.

There was nothing for it, Watson resolved. If he and Holmes were to avoid ending up in the Workhouse, the madness had to end. He'd have to demand that his companion abandon this folly. However, any possible stratagem for achieving this goal evaporated as a sudden scream disrupted his thoughts.

The wail of terror emanated from within, and bundling through the door he found Mrs Hudson, ashen faced and shrieking, pointing with trembling hands to the staircase carpet. Following her finger he gasped in apprehension.

A trail of droplets led up the gas-lit stairs, each tread soggy with an ominous splodge of viscous crimson. It didn't take much imagination to grasp its meaning and Watson bolted up the sticky steps two at a time.

Pulling out his service revolver, he gulped at what horrors he might encounter. The sight that presented itself made him gag with revulsion. The apartment was bloody, every inch, every cranny splattered and criminally despoiled.

And standing in the middle of the mayhem, clutching a dripping vermilion roller, Sherlock Holmes – once master detective but now self-proclaimed Greatest Interior Designer in the World – beamed with opium-fuelled satisfaction.

"Behold, behold," he proclaimed. "No longer an office in off-white, a living room in boring beige, but a study in scarlet."

For a second Watson considered shooting his crazed friend. He now understood what it meant to see red.

Yet, Holmes appeared oblivious, dropping the roller and snatching up a bright yellow brush.

"There's just time to give the porch one swift coat of canary before Inspector Lestrade pops round," he announced breathlessly.

Groaning, the doctor realised he didn't need to ask what glossy vandalism Sherlock intended for the hallway. He'd heard it dozens of times already.

"Lemon entry, my dear Watson. Lemon entry!"

Virgin Territory

Startled, Elaine grabbed the strap as the helicopter abruptly banked, plunging downwards towards the shimmering sheet of blue. She cursed, the unexpected motion making her stomach lurch violently.

God, she hated flying.

"Survey ship's about four miles away. Just over there. Due South. See." The pilot jabbed a gloved finger towards the distant shape silhouetted against the horizon.

Screwing up her eyes at the dazzling sunlight bouncing off the vast expanse of cyan, she recognised the familiar outline of Poseidon's Quest riding up and down on the gentle swell and felt some of her tension ease. Within a minute or two she'd be safely on the landing pad at the rear of the anchored research vessel – free of this rickety, rackety, levitating tin-can.

Even from this far out she could see the ship's crane swung out over the side, gingerly lowering the mini sub towards the waters of the Indian Ocean. It was nearly 4pm – the last dive of the afternoon; the last of five challenging daily submersions for the robot exploration pod, sending it hundreds of feet below the waves.

The derrick crew would be tired, but she knew they'd still be alert, cautious, taking huge care not to make any mistakes. Fatigue was dangerous and any lapse in concentration could bring the tiny craft – slowly swinging and rotating – smashing against the large ship's hull like a gleeful wrecking ball.

"I expect you'll be glad to get back to the action," the pilot commented, voice crackling on the headset microphone. "I really envy you. Searching for Atlantis. Wow, talk about a larger-than-life adventure. That must be mind blowing."

She nodded distractedly.

"It would be if we'd found anything," she agreed. "But so far it's been nothing but eight months of sweat, tears and frustration. Not a scrap of evidence, not a single artifact. Zip."

"But you're definitely on the right track? I heard it's only a matter of time. On the TV news last night they said your team is going to make a dramatic breakthrough any day now."

Despite her aerial jitters, and the acid churning in her belly, Elaine allowed herself a wry smile.

She'd heard that announcement too. Read all the upbeat, hyped, attention-grabbing write-ups. Alas, it was just publicity spin, something to keep the media happy and focused on the underwater archaeological expedition.

That was Richard's doing. The British tycoon wanted headlines and wasn't averse to putting a very rosy gloss on what was increasingly looking to be a PR disaster. He was paying for all this – to the tune of 2 million dollars a week – and wouldn't accept that the seabed scans and satellite imaging had come up blank; not so much as a sunken wreck, never mind a lost continent.

"But it's there," he'd told her just forty-eight hours ago at the crisis meeting in London. "Atlantis is down there. I just know it. It's simply a question of keeping faith. Widen the search area. Look harder. Work harder."

But they needed more than faith – they needed hard scientific proof. And as the chopper swung over the ship and began to land, Elaine told herself that this quixotic quest was rapidly turning into what the Brits called 'A Mug's Game'.

* * *

It had all seemed so different back in April when she'd been invited (she preferred to think of it as *summoned*) to the billionaire's Oxfordshire stately home. Then she'd been excited, optimistic and intensely curious.

Richard had been his famous charming, hyperactive, buoyant schoolboy self as he pumped her hand, dragged her inside and gushed: "Doctor Zuckerman. I can't begin to tell you what a real thrill it is to meet you. I've heard so much about your work on uncovering the treasures of ancient Troy. I've followed your career with huge interest."

"Call me Elaine," she'd replied, "and I have to admit I've heard a great deal about you too."

Mostly, she recalled, his exploits trying to kill himself in a series of increasingly dangerous daredevil publicity stunts – the last of which involved going over Niagara Falls in a barrel painted in his company's distinctive colours.

They'd taken afternoon tea in the huge wood-panelled library, she marvelling at the vast shelves of antique leather-bound books stretching thirty feet to the vaulted ceiling – and awed by how one of the world's richest men could be so badly dressed.

After twenty minutes or so of chit chat with him trying to convince her that hot air ballooning wasn't really as frightening or suicidal as she assumed, he got down to business.

"So, Doctor Zuckerman," he began, tone suddenly becoming firmer.

"It's Elaine."

"Yes, of course. Elaine. Tell me, how much do you know about Atlantis?"

She'd spluttered, almost spilling her cup of Earl Grey.

"Atlantis?"

"Yes. Atlantis. You know, the Lost Continent?"

Blinking, she'd studied his face to see if this was some bizarre test or that he was joking, recalling that Richard was almost as famous for his wicked sense of humour as his entrepreneurial genius. But he was deadly earnest, eyes shining brightly.

"Well, just what most classical scholars claim," she replied with a shrug. "That it was an advanced prehistoric civilisation, dating back to around 9600 BC. Legend has it that it was destroyed in a single day and night and disappeared beneath the waves never to be seen again."

"Yes, yes, the general myth is well known but what do you understand more specifically… as a scientist? As an expert in antiquity, an authority in early cities and ancient cultures?"

She made a dismissive face. "That it is a fairy tale, a fable. It never existed. It's a bedtime story dreamt up by Plato. He described it as the Isle of Atlas. I'm hazy on the exact details but there was some tie-up to Greek gods and magic. Allegedly, the inhabitants had advanced technology powered by some mysterious energy crystals."

She added: "Those who are gullible enough to believe the yarn claim the missing kingdom is located somewhere in the far northern Atlantic Ocean. But I've heard others put forward notions about it lying anywhere from the Azores to the Bahamas. And that's not including all the crackpot conspiracy theorists who will tell you it's everywhere from the North Pole to hidden underneath Central Park."

"And you don't buy into it – any of it?" he prompted.

"Sorry. I'm a scientist. I deal in facts. Verifiable facts. I put Atlantis in the same file as The Loch Ness Monster, UFOs and The Abominable Snowman. The one marked Freaky Fantasies."

At that the tycoon had suddenly laughed, and swung back on his chair. "Freaky Fantasies – I like that. That is so droll, so American," he chortled.

And, with an exuberant crash, he leapt to his feet.

"But what if I were to tell you that Atlantis really existed. That it isn't make-believe. What would you say if I told you that I have evidence that proves it; that I know where it is located?"

"I'd say," Elaine commented, refilling her cup and biting into one of the dainty cucumber sandwiches, "that you obviously had a bad bump on the head when you went over those falls."

* * *

Then he'd shown her the relic – had let her examine the intriguing tablet – and her whole world turned upside down.

The carved inscription wasn't Greek, wasn't Sanskrit, Latin or Egyptian but some strange hybrid – an ancient Esperanto. It featured many words she recognised, but many she didn't, and hieroglyphs, lots of them – arrays of small, crude, primitive pictograms.

"It's a hoax," she'd declared, unwilling to accept what her eyes were telling her. "It's impossible. I'm familiar with every known language of the Ancient World and I've never seen anything remotely like it before."

Running a finger thoughtfully over the bumps and dips of the stone, the billionaire nodded.

"That's what I thought at first," he confided, "I told myself it had to be a fake. It was too fanciful an idea to countenance. But then I let the lab boys loose on it."

"And?"

"And they were stunned. Completely bewildered. It passed every test they could throw at it – in fact, every test known to modern science."

The rock had been carved 10,000 years ago, using tools typical of the period, they'd deduced. The weathering was consistent with its age, and chemical erosion analysis showed the tablet had been immersed in salt water for millennia – then lain for further centuries in a hot climate, in sand with an acidic PH factor. And there were twenty-three other indicators to its provenance.

"The results were conclusive. Irrefutable," he gushed. "It's genuine. It's the real deal."

She couldn't accept it. Okay, so it was a clever fake, a clever old fake, but it still defied rational explanation. Surely Richard, with his legendary hard nose and business savvy, could see this.

"All right, then. Let's say that it is as old as you claim. Where was it found?" she challenged. "How did it come to light? I haven't heard anything about any centuries-old language tablet being uncovered. And, trust me, it's not something that would pass unnoticed."

He'd smiled mysteriously. "It popped up in the Middle East, about three years ago, on an old Grecian trade route. I won't go into details. It's best that you don't know the circumstances in which I acquired it. Let's just say that the downfall of a certain dictator helped a little."

Shaking her head, Elaine wondered who was more crazy – him for buying the counterfeit artifact or her, a serious scientist, for remaining there to listen to more of the madness. But, there were so many questions that intrigued her – nagging, puzzling questions – like what the Hell did the carving have to do with Plato's famous drowned-realm folk tale?

"That part is simple," he'd explained animatedly. "The language nerds have had a tough time deciphering the syntax and grammar, and some of the hieroglyphs are still a mystery, but the super computers have translated enough to identify that it's a set of directions. The tablet is a route map to the lost kingdom."

He pointed excitedly to a pictogram of a mermaid, the classic representation of the fabled sunken domain, then indicated the symbol next to it.

"It says Java," he said in an awed hush. "The location of Atlantis – lost to mankind for ten millennia – is off the coast of Indonesia. And guess what, Doctor Zuckerman. That's where you're headed. Freaky fantasy or not, you're going to find it for me."

* * *

Watching the chopper disappearing into the distance, Elaine rubbed her brow. Another headache was coming, a result of all the noise, vibrations and diesel fumes.

"London meeting go well?"

She turned and offered a sour grimace to Neil. Her deputy project leader, grunted knowingly.

"Oh, that bad," he surmised.

"Worse," Elaine replied, as they made their way from the swaying helipad and down the narrow gangway to the main deck of the survey ship. "Richard was doing his nut. He's a man used to getting his way. And he simply refuses to believe he could be wrong."

"So what do we do?"

"Keep looking," Elaine concluded with a sigh. "Keep scouring the area for any clue. Keep going until we either find something or he grows bored of the whole escapade and calls it off."

Neil looked at her as though she was a naïve child. "Call it off? He's not going to do that any time soon. His whole reputation hangs on us succeeding. Besides, I've heard he's already made plans to turn it into a vast sub-aqua theme park."

He put on a passable limey accent: "Bring the whole family to the historical holiday of a lifetime at Atlantis-land. The Underwater Magic Kingdom."

Despite herself, Elaine smiled.

"C'mon – let's duck into the control room," she suggested. "The camera link from the mini-sub should be online by now. Maybe just maybe, this time there'll be something – anything – that we can point to as progress."

The interior of the main cabin was eerily dark, the only illumination coming from the radar and the viewing screens. The slouching technicians nodded a greeting for an instant before returning to boredly scrutinising the grainy images coming from the depths. Visibility wasn't great; swirling sand and sediment making the water a cloudy, foggy mass of tiny dancing dots.

A shark swam into view, investigating the robot pod for a few seconds, before darting away. Two stray lobsters crawled across the undulating ocean floor.

Then nothing.

It was just the same as every other dive. No roadways or ruins, no temples or toppled statues. No sign of civilisation. Zero. Nada. Zilch.

Even the sound of the sonar pinging off the sub to the seabed seemed forlorn and dispirited, as though it knew how futile it all was.

Wherever it lay – fact or fable – Atlantis was obviously nowhere near Java, even if the jewel of the Indian Ocean was the most populated island in the world, sitting in the most densely inhabited region on the planet. Even if the isle was one of the most ancient sites of human activity.

"There's no point me waiting around here. I'm going to crash out for a few hours," Elaine announced with a loud yawn. "The jet lag is kicking in."

She turned to leave, when there was a noise. A loud buzz. A loud, insistent buzz – the satellite phone.

Groaning, she told Neil: "I can guess who that is. For Heaven's sake, what does he expect. I've just got back. I know he's frustrated with us but I can't perform miracles."

Aware that everyone was listening in, she said: "I'll take this in my cabin."

Safely alone, she dropped angrily into a chair and stabbed the button that activated the microwave video-link phone and its webcam.

Richard's face appeared on the screen, movements jerky through the time delay.

He had an expression she'd never seen before – a strange mixture of glee, disappointment, smug secrecy and open wonder. It was disconcerting. She wondered vaguely if the stress had finally got to him.

"Hi, Elaine," he said, voice sounding even more fatigued than hers. "I bet you weren't expecting to hear from me again so soon."

"No," she said, popping the ring pull on a Diet Pepsi and taking a swig. "I wasn't, and I know you're not going to be pleased but I have to tell you that I don't have any update. The status of the project is unchanged. Atlantis is not just a lost continent – it's a lost cause."

She expected some outburst, at least a curse, but the tycoon nodded as if it was exactly what he'd anticipated – and that he didn't mind.

"Yes, well, frankly that's not surprising. Not in the circumstances," he said, licking his lips both nervously and with excitement.

She stopped in mid slurp, puzzled. "Richard?"

"That's why I'm phoning. I've got some news." He smiled, sheepishly. "But you're not going to like it. There's been a... development."

For an instant, Doctor Elaine Zuckerman felt more alert, more tense and more worried than she'd ever been in her life.

"What kind of development?" she demanded.

"It's a breakthrough." He made a vague wobbling gesture with his hand. "Well, more of a re-evaluation."

At that moment, if she could have leapt forward, grabbed him by the throat and shaken him, she would have. Instead, she made do with hissing: "What? What are you saying? What am I not going to like? Spit it out."

He paused, breathed in deeply and said: "The language geeks have finally cracked the code on the tablet. And it's not what we thought."

Not, what you thought, she muttered darkly under her breath.

"The inscription is undoubtedly ancient. It does date back to when we calculated, but it isn't directions to Atlantis. In fact, it turns out it doesn't refer to the bloody place at all."

"So what does it refer to?" she said through gritted teeth, mentally adding up the man hours, the astronomical costs and the damage to her scientific reputation that the wild goose chase had clocked up.

"Well, this is the funny bit – and it will make you laugh. But it turns out it's actually a pre-history sales pitch, a sort of early newspaper advertisement."

An advertisement! An advert! She'd trekked half way across the globe and wasted most of a year for a bloody leaflet!

So what in the name of everything holy was the tablet advertising?

He giggled, then stopped suddenly and frowned. "Well, let's just say that a certain Seattle company hasn't exactly been telling the truth about when they first launched."

* * *

"I don't believe it," Neil gasped.

"Neither do I, but apparently it's the truth," Elaine confirmed minutes later. "And it all makes sense when you put it together – the mermaid picture and the symbol for Java."

"But the media are going to tear Richard apart when they get wind that the whole quest was based on a monumental mistake. He'll be ruined; a laughing stock."

Smiling ruefully, Elaine nodded. "Maybe, maybe not. Something tells me, he'll turn it round. By the time he's dropped his 10,000-year-old bombshell no-one will even care about the Atlantis fiasco. It'll be forgotten."

She leant across to switch on the TV. The newsflash was due any second. Richard was about to spill the beans.

It was destined to be the story of the decade. Something they'd all be talking about for the rest of their lives. Something that would rewrite the history books.

He was about to tell the world that the artifact actually said: *"Drink At Starbucks – best skinny latte in Antiquity."*

Poet Tree in Moh-Shan

The ride took three hard days – a bone-jarring 150-mile gallop across desert, scrubland and raging streams.

Under the merciless baking sun, Gregg had cursed for agreeing to the exhausting, quixotic trek through bandit country, and for what? A silly, senseless, romantic gesture.

But Li Yew had been insistent. His new girlfriend yearned to see the famed willow – to put its fabled talent to the ultimate test – and if he wanted her, he had to make the sacred pilgrimage.

"In the days of my ancestors, lovers would come to the tree to gain its blessing for their union," she'd explained. "And I cannot give my love to any man without us doing the same."

Okay, what harm could it do, he'd reasoned. They'd stare at the tree for a few minutes, leave some hokey token to the gods, and then he'd get roaring drunk.

She'd be happy, he'd be off the hook and maybe – just maybe – his fragrant, fragile, tiny, prudish blossom would finally let him into her bed.

Poor, silly, gullible, superstitious Li Yew believed that the mystical tree could see into your soul; that it knew your innermost thoughts and motives.

"And I suppose it talks," he'd teased.

"Yes," she'd replied softly. "In a way it does. It sings to you, in rhyme. As the wind rustles through its leaves, you can hear its message…"

The idea was clearly preposterous, a con to lure credulous tourists, but Gregg wasn't going to risk weeks of carnal delights by pointing this out.

And his lust surged as the horses rounded the bend and it appeared at last, bowed by the river's edge; the legendary Poet Tree.

Li Yew dropped from the saddle and ran forward, unable to contain her excitement.

Bowing before the delicate, revered willow she closed her eyes. For a second or two nothing happened, then the leaves rustled as though a mighty breeze had swept past.

Stunned, Gregg realised he could hear words, faint, whispered, lyrical words:

Li Yew – gentlest heart, take care

beware the forlorn bliss,

revealing the tender betrayal

of a scheming lover's kiss.

Shaking his head, Gregg told himself he was imagining it – hallucinating after days of sun. Yet no matter how crazy, how impossible, the tree was talking. And it was warning about him!

In an instant, everything he understood changed. Standing in this magical, bewildering, ancient spot, under the mighty willow's searching arboreal gaze, he felt reborn, renewed, all cynicism washed away.

Seeing the hope in Li Yew's face, he stepped forward, silently praying that the Poet Tree would find him worthy; would forgive his laddish, boozing, raucous, sexually obsessed ways and see the true beauty and compassion in his soul.

The willow swayed... and moaned... and creaked, the sad, drooping branches swishing backwards and forwards. It looked deep inside him and saw... and the whispering supernatural leaves spoke:

There was a young girl from Beijing

Who got knocked up in a fling...

Just Imagine

Murmurs of discontent swept the capacity audience. Peeping round the curtains, Roddy McPherson studied the anxious faces and grinned, savouring their tension.

The rows of annoyed delegates fidgeted, fearful that he wasn't going to appear – or worse, be so drunk he'd stagger across the stage and slur incoherently, unable to deliver his keynote speech.

After all, it had happened before...

It was that sense of danger, the unpredictability of what the bourbon-swigging hell-raiser would do or say, which had attracted so many to the symposium. That and the fact that the bad boy of speculative fiction sold more books than the rest of the genre's masters put together.

"Please, Mr McPherson – I'm pleading. The MC has announced you twice already," the organiser's voice grew so high-pitched that it could shatter glass.

"And he can do it a third time," Roddy replied, unconcerned. "I like hearing people mention my name."

"But the schedule! The delegates have planes to catch, hotel rooms to vacate. You're throwing the whole conference into chaos."

Putting an arm round the panicking official, he guided the man towards the crack in the drapes.

"See those people. My rivals. They'll wait. Trust me, for the great Roddy McPherson, they'll wait forever. They want to know my secret. They yearn to understand how the Mozart of modern sci-fi does it."

"Yes, yes, I appreciate that. That's why we booked you – at such expense. But why the unnecessary delay in taking the stage?"

Roddy beamed. "Because it's showbiz. All part of the magic. I intend to make a dramatic entrance; to build up the expectation to bursting point."

The man frowned disapprovingly, but Roddy ignored him. Sensing the optimum moment had come, he was already striding towards the podium, waving to the hordes who leapt to their feet, exploding in spontaneous and relieved applause.

Bowing, he winked – giving them the full mega-watt effect of his famous Celtic smile.

"Please, please," he purred. "You're too kind. Please. You're making me blush. I'm just a humble writer…"

In a ten thousand dollar suit.

He waited until the delegates were back on their seats – on the edge of their seats – before saying: "Now, I'm going to ditch the pleasantries and the platitudes and all the other bullshit that you've been forced to listen to for the last few days and get straight to the point. I'll answer the big question. Why am I so successful?"

He leant forward conspiratorially.

"It's very simple," he said, barely above a whisper, causing the masses to topple alarmingly as they strained to listen. "I've liberated myself. I've thrown off the shackles, restrictions and formulas of orthodox storytelling. It may be ironic to reveal it at a narrative convention, but I've stopped obeying normal narrative conventions."

He scanned the hall for several long moments, enjoying the bafflement that radiated back.

Build up the tension, Roddy boy, tease their curiosity, make them sweat...

"I have abandoned using the 'what if?' principle in my work," he announced.

The next two minutes were bedlam as the audience reeled, unsure if he was mocking them or had simply lost his mind.

"But that's ridiculous," one voice shouted angrily. "It's impossible to write a sci-fi story without using what if?"

"It's the whole basis of what we do," another agreed. "It's the trigger question that fires the imagination; the crucial key that unlocks reality and makes anything possible in a fantasy tale."

Delighting at the stunned response and the headlines the controversy would undoubtedly generate, Roddy signalled for quiet.

"I can see I've stirred up a hornets' nest," he observed. "But I promise you it is possible to exist without it. Asking readers to imagine what if? is a cheap trick, a lazy device."

He sighed theatrically. "But, I can see you don't believe me, so indulge me in a small experiment. Close your eyes and imagine my world for a moment. Imagine – what if the what if? principle had never been invented."

There was resistance; many suspecting this was some huge practical joke, but gradually all complied. And Roddy closed his eyes too.

Silence fell across the hall.

A total silence.

An eerie silence.

Opening his lids after several moments, Roddy glanced out – into rows and rows of vacant seats.

His mouth fell open.

He was alone, but for an elderly man in a security uniform, hand half way to his holster.

"What you doing here, mister?" the guard demanded.

Roddy couldn't answer. His brain couldn't take it in.

Spinning round, first one way then the other, he stared frantically at the empty hall. It was impossible. Where were the people? And why was he now bafflingly dressed in threadbare jeans and sweatshirt?

"I'm – I'm here for the conference," he gasped, waving a hand helplessly.

The man had his gun out now, warily edging forwards. "Ain't no convention here, bud. Building should be all locked up."

"But – but that's crazy. It was here. Just seconds ago. I was the guest speaker, for Heaven's sake. I was talking to my fellow science fiction authors."

The guard's next three words were chilling as, eyes narrowing, he demanded: "What's science fiction?"

Roddy teetered on the edge of madness. Then he laughed – long and hard as he suddenly understood that the others had been right. They really couldn't exist without their precious what if?

Shrugging at the watchman, he considered the challenge of convincing anyone that there'd been a world where sane people earned a living from dreaming up stories about space ships, little green men, robots, time travel and alternative realities. A world that had vanished a mere moment before.

No-one would believe it. It sounded too far-fetched, too fanciful. But yet, the great Roddy McPherson thought he might just be able to pull it off.

"Look," he said, turning on the twinkle. "Just imagine for a moment..."

CS–Aye, Jimmy

There was no doubt about it, Frodo Baggins was dead. The diminutive fellow was both frigid and rigid – hairy bare feet sticking out from under the huge rock that had flattened him.

"Looks like mordor," DCI Matt Burke told his team of Caledonian detectives as they surveyed the crime scene.

"No, sir," DS Jackie Reid immediately corrected her boss, nodding to the otherwise idyllic fields and cottages. "I think you'll find this is The Shire."

Frowning in annoyance, the Glaswegian top cop adjusted his accent. "I mean, it's murrr-der," he explained. "There's nae way this could have been an accident."

His crack polis team all nodded in agreement. Partly because the way the tiny brutalised body was lying suggested Frodo had been the victim of considerable violence, partly because challenging the boss' opinion wasn't a good idea – but mostly because any suggestion of it being a death by natural causes and they were on the next bus home. And all had yet to visit The Mines of Moria, take holiday snaps on Mount Doom or sample a meal in the revolving restaurant at the top of Saruman's tower.

Admittedly, at first they'd been reluctant to take the posting, until the Super explained they were going to be assigned to Middle Earth – not Middle England. But now the tartan 'tecs were desperate to spin out their secondment to this blighted continent with its casual violence, bitter devastation, inhuman creatures and sudden death. It was, they agreed, a more genteel, conducive and welcoming environment than their normal Clydeside beat...

Years of intensively honed investigative experience meant the DCI's keen mind was already whirring wildly with questions. What was the motive? Who had the means? Were there any witnesses? And why was his show called Taggart when that wasn't his name?

"Was it robbery?" he asked, reminding himself wisely that it was probably better to be known as a Taggart than a Burke. "Somedae's nicked the wee yin's shoes."

"He didn't wear any," Sergeant Reid told him wearily, slowly letting her eyeballs rise skyward.

No shoes! Jezz, Burke told himself, now that's what I call a hard man.

"But he is missing some jewellery," the sergeant added and the DCI's estimation of Frodo dipped in an instant.

"Jewellery? What kind – gold chains? Bracelet? A watch? Not ear-rings – tell me it's nae ear-rings!"

She didn't answer, but led her superior officer to the group of suspects – a dwarf, an elegant elf, a goblin with a perm, a shifty looking nomadic wanderer and a hideous slime-covered orc. Burke couldn't explain why but the line-up reminded him of a boy band.

"These are his mates," Reid informed him, looking at her notes. "They call themselves The Fellowship of the Bling. They say he should have been wearing a ring of some sort. It's gone."

A missing ring, eh?

The DCI suspiciously eyed the rather colourful-looking fellows of the Fellowship. What a bunch of vain Jessies! Any one of these fancy dress poseurs could have nicked it, he told himself. Maybe jealousy over the jewellery had sparked a row amongst the group – a tiff over who wore the Tiffany?

"It was a very special ring," the Elf interrupted his musing, voice unexpectedly deep and mellow. "The one ring – the one ring to bind them all. The Dark Lord's ring."

Burke let that unexpected nugget percolate around his grey matter. This put a whole new complexion on the case.

"I see, so it was an engagement ring," he deduced, snapping his fingers triumphantly. "Frodo was supposed to marry the Dark Lord. And they had a lover's quarrel."

He nodded sagely. "Aye, that'll be it. Some men seem to think putting a ring on your finger means they can control you. The wee yin probably ditched him, called off the wedding, threw the ring back at him. The Dark Lord was crushed so he thought Frodo should be too."

A domestic crime, a gay domestic. Well, that shouldn't be too difficult to clear up, he thought with relief.

The Elf looked helplessly at DS Reid. She just shrugged back. She'd only had one grudging promotion in twenty-five years and more than ninety-five episodes. Why should she stick her neck out?

A scream broke the embarrassed silence.

"The precious! The precious! He's got the precious. Nasty, horrible brute... he's got the precious and we wants it!"

The entire team of detectives spun round to look at the pathetic, emaciated, stick-like creature that was jumping up and down in rage; lank strands of greasy hair falling down over his grey face and shrunken mad, sly eyes.

"Somehow I don't think this is going to make things any better," Reid groaned.

Gollum was pointing accusingly at Gandalf the Grey – who was walking surreptitiously in the opposite direction, whistling innocently, magical staff in one hand and the strap of his pull-along wheelie suitcase in the other.

"See, see. He's creeping away. Nasty, wicked wizard. Killed master Frodo, took the precious, he did. Took our precious. Give it back, give it back to Sméagol."

Shock swept across the mighty sorcerer's face, and switched instantly to fury.

"Sméagol? Sneak-le, more like!" he roared bitterly, quickly hiding the ring in his pocket. "You grass! Why couldn't you have kept your big trap shut? Another minute and I'd have been free and clear."

Turning the staff on the woe-begotten wretch, he hissed: "Well, I can make you quiet now. You won't be giving evidence against me."

There was a sharp, electric crack and the unmistakable odour of ozone. Gollum's mouth was certainly shut – it was gone, vanished. A blank space now sat on his face where his lips had been.

DCI Burke cursed. That bit of grievous bodily charm had silenced his only witness to the slaying. It would make the trial trickier, he realised, but they'd just have to worry about that problem when Gandalf was safely in custody.

With a nod, he signalled his men to make the arrest.

Alas, the booming, bearded, buccaneer of black magic wasn't coming quietly.

They barely had time to react before Gandalf used his sizzling cane again. With a non-audible eye-bulging yelp, Gollum was compacted into a tight ball and bowled straight into the detectives and the Fellowship of the Bling standing behind them.

"Stri-kkkke," the wizard shouted gleefully as the ten figures toppled in unison.

Picking themselves up, Burke and Reid surged forward but weren't quick enough. With speed remarkable for such an elderly figure, the enchanter swept the oversized wand in a circle – causing a three-feet-high wall of fire to surround him.

"You shall not pass," he warned, from behind the protective flames.

"Look, pal," Burke began, keeping his voice calm and soothing. "No-one blames you. It's tough when your pension doesn't go as far as you'd expected. We all ken that... but this isnae the answer."

"You could let me go," Gandalf suggested. "You have no DNA, fingerprints, fibres – no proof at all. Besides, this isn't really your jurisdiction."

The DCI shook his head regretfully. "Sorry, there's nae way. You've got to be stopped. You've killed one wee man. What if you killed another? And a third? Before you know it you'd be murrr-dering them every week. I cannae let you make a hobbit of it."

Nearby, Jackie Reid muttered: "Oh my Goad!" but Burke couldn't tell if it was in exasperation at the stand-off or the awfulness of the pun.

He didn't have a chance to ask.

Reaching into her bag, his sergeant produced a metal object and – without a moment's hesitation – threw it. Spinning end over end, the orange-coloured missile flew swiftly over the fiery barrier and hit Gandalf squarely between the eyes.

The can of Irn-Bru did its work and the concussed wizard went down like a Sauchiehall Street drunk.

"Magic," Reid said, with a self-satisfied smirk.

With Gandalf out for the count, the flames immediately died down.

"Get the cuffs on him," Burke ordered his officers, stretching his hand into the comatose magician's pocket and producing the cause of all the troubles.

The ring was so slight. Was it really worth killing for?

It looked normal, apart from some weird writing inside. But it felt... it felt different...

Strange thoughts raced through Burke's mind – long forgotten feelings of ambition, greed, ruthlessness. Why shouldn't he be Chief Constable? Commissioner of the Met? Overlord of all beings!!!!

"We'll definitely need to get a confession now that Gollum can't speak," Jackie Reid pointed out.

But Burke already had deliciously inventive, diabolical, sadistic ideas ricocheting round his brain. Locking up the wizard in a dark, deep, dank cell... playing him the bagpipes all night... forcing him to watch Monarch of the Glen... feeding him a merciless diet of haggis and deep-fried Mars Bars.

"Don't you worry," he informed his deputy with evil certainly. "I ken exactly how to make him crack. He'll be tolkien before he knows it."

Cheater

After two weeks searching, I finally see him – three cars ahead. Tonight is the night, I tell myself excitedly. Tonight I teach the fat, ignorant slob the lesson of his life.

He turns into the supermarket car park, and I'm following 50 yards back – waiting for him to do it again. And yes, there he goes. Straight into the designated spot by the door, parking his enormous rust bucket up the middle of two marked disabled spaces.

I'm seething, breath coming in short gasps. How dare he! He's not disabled, not even the slightest limp, just too obese and arrogant to bother parking where he should.

He's typical of people these days, nothing but contempt. No thought for anyone else. Another yob giving two fingers to the system. Another cheater.

But tonight it ends.

As he goes into the shop, I park my car across the end of his – making a T-shape.

He's trapped and I'm waiting when he comes out. His squat, podgy face is surprised then enraged. His stomach ripples like jelly under his cheap rugby shirt.

"What the f... do you think you're doing," he yells. "You're boxing me in. Move your bloody wreck out of my way."

I shake my head and move closer, waving my blue disabled badge at him. Now the cheater knows what's going on. It makes him even angrier, a stream of abuse pouring out.

He wants to hit me, except you can't hit a man on crutches. Even a yob has his limits...

But I don't, and he's stunned when I let the crutches fall and take my first swing. My fist lands dead centre on his face, and I hear a satisfying crunch when I make contact with his nose.

Then I hit him again and again and again ... all my fury and sense of injustice powering the blows.

Not the cripple he was expecting. Now maybe he'll think twice before parking in the disabled spot – MY spot.

As I bend to retrieve the sticks, I give him a kick for good measure. I'm feeling good – he won't go to the cops, won't snitch. Who'd believe him?

Then, unexpectedly, I sense someone watching nearby. Is it the police? No, it's a different van. It's the one that I've seen around. Like when I was at the rec playing footie yesterday afternoon.

There's a man in a suit, and another with a video camera. The ID badge bears the symbol of the Department for Health and Pensions.

"Bit of a show you put on there, Mr Carter," the rat-faced official tells me. "Not bad for a man on incapacity benefit; someone who is supposed to be bent over with back pain."

I think to lie, make up some excuse, but I can tell they won't be fooled.

As I walk back to the van with them, the cameraman looks me up and down with contempt.

"I hate cheaters," he mutters.

Crazy Paving

Elsie stopped pruning her roses to watch the small flat-bed builder's truck cruising up the street. She trembled as it pulled up at the foot of her driveway with a menacing hiss.

"Watchya, grandma," a cheery voice called out from inside the cab. "Is your old man in? We need a word with him."

She shook her head. "N-n-no," she stammered. "He's gone. D-d-dead. I'm on my own now."

The truck doors opened and two young lads – Elsie guessed they were in their early twenties – leapt out.

"In that case," the taller one said, "it's you we want then. It's about your driveway."

Elsie frowned. "My driveway. What about my driveway?"

"It's dangerous," the second lad told her. "An absolute disgrace. Have you seen the state of it?"

"Dangerous?" Elsie repeated slowly. "Disgrace?"

"Yeah," the first lad told her animatedly. "Potentially lethal. We noticed it as we drove by. I said to Terry, that driveway is a potential killer. If some young kiddie was to trip in one of those potholes we could be talking about a death. Didn't I say that, Terry?"

Stern-faced, Terry nodded. "You did, Wayne. You most certainly did."

"So," Wayne continued, putting on his best sincere smile, "we thought to ourselves. How lucky. What a coincidence. We just happen to have a load of fresh tarmac in the back of the van."

"Ready for laying," Terry added helpfully.

"Ready for laying," Wayne agreed. "And we thought, why not see if we could do you a favour and repair your driveway at a very reasonable charge – making it safe for all the children in the street and saving you the hassle and inconvenience of having to phone round contractors for a load of stupid old quotes you don't need."

Elsie blinked. She didn't know what to think. The postman HAD tripped in the driveway just the other day. So had that nice woman from Age Concern who'd come to tell her something about bogus builders.

She stared at the pockmarked tarmac. The driveway did look awful. She'd let things go a bit since George had passed on. He'd handled all that side of things and now he was gone she was totally adrift – baffled by life's many complexities. Her gaze moved up to the two lads, both standing looking strangely angelic and caring.

She smiled. It would be great to get the driveway fixed, and having Wayne and Terry do it would mean that she wouldn't fall prey to those nasty cowboys who were touring the neighbourhood.

"Okay," she said after a few moments. "I don't see what harm it can do."

"Great," Terry said happily. "We'll get cracking, grandma. Why don't you nip inside and make us all a nice cup of tea?"

* * *

As she waited for the kettle to boil, Elsie hunted for her tablets. She was getting one of her headaches – the ones that came whenever she forgot to take her medication; the headache she'd had when she pushed poor old George off the ladder.

The psychiatric report had been full of long words, words she couldn't understand. They'd said something about her being a pavement or something like that. She hadn't taken much notice.

The fresh-faced doctor, straight from medical college, had convinced the others that she was safe to rejoin society. There was no chance of her displaying any more anti-social tendencies.

"Elsie Watts is just what she appears to be – a sweet, silver-haired, pensioner," he'd said. "I'm convinced the whole business with the ladder was a one-off incident. She no longer poses any real threat."

Elsie smiled at the memory. The doctor had been a nice boy – just like Terry and Wayne. She wondered if the three lads knew each other.

"Coo-ee," she cried through the window. "Tea's ready. Would you like a chocolate biscuit?"

Wayne, and Terry, grinning widely, nodded back. "We're almost done," they answered. "We'll have a nice cuppa... and you can get out your chequebook."

* * *

Gazing forlornly at the black, smelly, lumpy mess, Elsie couldn't help feeling she'd made a mistake, a terrible mistake.

"It's awful. What have you done?" she asked, stunned. "Look, there are dips in it. It's not flat."

Terry sniffed: "That's your sub-strata."

Wayne nodded: "Definitely. The land is an undulating mass of subterranean layers. You're lucky we got it as flat as we did. Normally we wouldn't tackle a tricky job like this one without a full survey team."

"And geological bore holes," Terry agreed.

Elsie wasn't convinced. The two builders had made the driveway look worse than before they'd started. Her headache pounded behind her eyes. She felt giddy.

Wayne waved a piece of white paper before her streaming eyes.

"What's this?" she asked worriedly.

"The bill," Terry replied, the helpful smile now vanished.

"For £4,000," Wayne told Elsie, his face coming up close to hers.

The world started to wobble in front of her. £4,000! She didn't have £4,000! They'd said it would be cheap. No-one said it would be that much. "I haven't got it," she croaked. "I'm just a poor pensioner."

"Tough," the contractors chorused. "You owe it and we're not budging till we get it."

Elsie started to shake uncontrollably. "You'd better watch out," she gasped. "I'm a dangerous woman. I'm a... I'm a... pavement."

The lads sniggered loudly. "And I'm a dual carriageway," Terry told her nastily. "Now get the money."

Dazed, she gestured for the two lads to follow her back inside the kitchen.

Elsie's heart thumped so loudly against her chest that she thought it would burst through. The room spun madly, the wind rushed in her ears. She couldn't stop herself. Suddenly, she knew what she had to do. The bread knife was close... so close.

* * *

Even though she was no builder, Elsie thought she'd done a good job of levelling out the dips in the driveway. The two bodies had fitted the holes a treat.

Now that the task was done the tarmac didn't look too bad. No-one would be tripping over any more.

She hummed happily to herself as she washed the blood-stained bread knife in the sink. The headache had gone, just as it had done when George's nagging was silenced.

Without the pain in her head, Elsie could think a little clearer. She could remember what the psychiatric report had said. It hadn't called her a pavement – of course not. That would have been silly. It had called her a cycle path...

A Soonful of Spugar

The college doctor jumped. Who could be banging on his door at this time of night – and so insistently?

Hurrying to the porch, he was stunned to see the Dean there – looking pale and unsteady.

"My fear dellow, hank God you're tear," his caller gushed, grabbing his lapels, obviously dazed and confused. "I heed your nelp. I seem to be muffering from some sadness. I keep wuddling my mords."

The doctor blinked in surprise, not sure if his ears were playing tricks. He'd never heard anything like it. What strange contagion of the mind was affecting Reverend William?

"Good Lord, man. You look awful. You'd better come in," he said, catching his colleague as the man stumbled.

"Lanks a thot," the distressed cleric said gratefully as he was guided to a chair and given a large brandy. "You're kost mind."

The doctor listened carefully for several minutes as his distraught visitor babbled on bafflingly.

"It's a bizarre condition," he mused. "You appear to be transposing the openings to adjacent words. You're automatically creating a new vocabulary that is gibberish – but also comprehensible. I've never come across anything like it in all my years of medicine. What could have possibly caused this?"

The Dean pointed to the back of his skull. "I had a hump on the bed," he informed his host. "Then I found myself locking like a tooney."

Ah, a bump on the head, the physician thought excitedly. That might do it. The brain was a delicate organ, easily disrupted.

"Do you think you might be having a nervous breakdown?" he ventured.

"A bervous neckdown? I don't think so," the worried clergyman replied. "Apart from muddling my words, I feel quite normal."

The doctor did a double take and eyed his friend suspiciously.

"You sounded unaffected there," he said accusingly. "That second sentence was perfectly understandable. There was no transposition."

"It gums and coes," the Dean explained, exasperated. "It's rompletely candom. But I've found that eating chint mochlete seems to help."

For the first time, the doctor noticed blood. The cranial injury was more severe than he'd thought. Opening his black bag, he found a bottle of iodine and began dabbling it on – aware of the Dean wincing at each touch.

"Does that hurt?" he enquired.

"Lust a jittle."

So what caused the bump? It was a particularly nasty wound, he observed.

"It was my wife," Reverend William confessed, red faced. "She pit me with a hoker. She caught me with my fit of bluff. Texy Sina!"

"Fit of bluff? Texy Sina? Ah, I see – she caught you with your bit of fluff. Sexy Tina!"

"Rat's tight!"

"And what had you done? With Sexy Tina? To provoke your wife to such violence with the poker?"

The Reverend William Archibald Spooner paused for a second, let a lecherous smile cross his lips and, for a fleeting moment of normality, replied: "I told you, Dear Doctor. I had a hump on the bed!"

Growing Out of Burgers

Guest story by Sally Jenkins

Madame Dupont whipped the egg and then poured the sunshine yellow liquid into a dish of raw minced beef. Lindsay watched as she bound the meat and egg together with the fork. The only noise was the occasional scrape of metal on glass.

He'd just got up and the house was empty apart from him and his hostess.

She caught his eye and gave him a knowing smile. It was 10am but she was still in her dressing-gown, not a huge fluffy candlewick thing like his mother wore but a thin, silky, red affair that was held together by a tie-belt. The gown was low-cut and Lindsay could see the flesh at the top of her bosoms. He knew he shouldn't look but that slight wobble of olive skin drew his eyes like a magnet. She must be naked under that dressing-gown and Lindsay had never seen a naked woman.

This school exchange visit was turning out better than he'd expected, given the bad start of the evening before.

French families had already claimed all his classmates. He'd been the only one left in the Lycee assembly hall.

"Lindsay Wilson?" the teacher had called at last.

"That's me." He stood up.

The teacher looked flummoxed. "You are a boy." She stated the obvious in heavily accented English. "I expected a girl."

"Lindsay can be a boy's or a girl's name." How many times in his 15 years had he given this explanation? Exactly the same number of times he'd cursed his parents for landing him with such a puffy name.

"But we have partnered you with a girl, Corinne Dupont, for the exchange holiday. This is not good."

A girl and a woman stood up on the far side of the hall.

"There is nowhere else for you to go," the teacher continued.

There was a hurried conversation between the teacher, the woman and the girl. Every few seconds the woman glanced sideways at Lindsay, as though she were inspecting him. Then she came and kissed him on each cheek.

"Bienvenue, Lindsay. I will like to have a man in the house. I will like to satisfy his appetite." She put an odd emphasis on this last word whilst looking him directly in the eye. "I am a good cook."

Lindsay felt his cheeks flush under her gaze.

She had to be Corinne's mother. But her face was unlike that of any mother he knew. There were no comfortable lines around the eyes or flashes of grey in her roots. This French mother had smooth olive skin, cropped black hair and her close fitting dress clung to a figure that was best described to others using cupped male hand movements.

"Salut!" Corinne had stepped forward to welcome him too. She was smaller, thinner and less sexy than her mother – but better than a lot of the girls in Lindsay's year at school. For a start she had no spots.

"Did you sleep well?"

The question jolted him back to the present. He lifted his eyes from Madame Dupont's flash of breast, which was wobbling with the exertion of working the fork in the meat.

"Yes, thank you."

It was a lie but what else could he say? When he'd arrived at the house the previous evening Madame Dupont had produced a bottle of fizzy wine, damp with condensation. The house had echoed to a gun-shot as she opened it.

"Let us celebrate a man in the house!" she said, handing Corinne a small glass.

Then she poured liberally into Lindsay's. The liquid frothed over and ran on to the table.

"We will be good together, n'est ce pas?" she said and clinked her flute to his. "A man in the house is good."

He raised the wet glass to his lips and sipped. The sour bubbles hit his nostrils and made him cough. Madame Dupont had already finished her wine. Lindsay felt obliged to follow suit and discovered that the quicker he drank, the more bearable it was. By the third glass he was high on the fizz as well as the way Madame Dupont was treating him as a valued adult male.

"Sleep," she announced, suddenly.

Lindsay tottered as he stood up and was surprised to find that the floor was no longer level. Then Madame Dupont's arm was around him. His nostrils were filled with her spicy perfume combined with a more earthy smell which he identified as female sweat. Surprisingly, it was exciting instead of revolting.

At the top of the stairs he glimpsed Corinne's large bedroom with two twin beds, both made up. Obviously the female Lindsay Wilson had been supposed to share a room with her exchange partner.

"We have another room," Madame Dupont said quickly, stopping Lindsay from following Corinne into her pink and white boudoir.

The other room was more like a broom cupboard. There was a fold-up camp bed leaning against the wall and Madame Dupont indicated that he should set it up. He was still struggling with the metal frame when she came back with a sleeping bag and pillow. She stood close to him and helped his fumbling hands to loosen the catch. He felt the heat of her body and the pressure of her limbs through his clothes.

Then she kissed him goodnight on the cheek. He tried to return the compliment but she had gone.

Afterwards he'd lain awake for ages, entertained by tantalising thoughts of his hostess. He'd tried to push her from his mind but his teenage hormones and wine befuddled brain hadn't let him.

Now he had a headache.

"You look tired," she said, taking the tall wooden pepper mill and twisting.

A shower of black dots floated into the pink meat. Her flesh wobbled again as she pressed the flavouring through the mixture. Lindsay fingered the mobile in his pocket and wondered if he could get a photo.

"You were still asleep when Corinne went to school. I thought it more important that you rested than had lessons."

"Merci." Lindsay was glad he hadn't been wakened – his dreams about a continental woman with short dark hair had been much better than a school desk.

Madame Dupont sat down opposite him and placed a forkful of the beef in her mouth. Lindsay's stomach turned. He'd thought she was preparing homemade burgers for lunch. Wouldn't she catch Mad Cow Disease or Foot and Mouth? Then there was the raw egg – his mother was always going on about salmonella.

The French woman was chewing slowly, obviously enjoying what was in her mouth. The smell of raw flesh wasn't mixing well with Lindsay's headache.

"Et tu?" she asked and offered him a forkful of the mixture.

At home with his own mother, he would have made throwing-up noises to show his revulsion at the food. Instead, he opened his mouth and she placed the fork into it.

His body tingled at the intimacy of sharing. It felt like they were lovers. At the same time he was fighting not to gag on the raw meat as he chewed it and prepared to swallow. It was the consistency rather than the peppery taste that disagreed with him.

"More?" She refilled the fork and was offering it again.

He opened his lips and she slipped it in, smiling.

"You are a proper man," she said. "My husband must have it cooked. But you do not fear disease."

Lindsay sat up taller at her words and tried to appear more macho than the gangly youth that he was. He swallowed the uncooked flesh quickly.

"Where is Monsieur Dupont?" He tried to keep his voice casual.

"In Dubai. I am alone for now." She uttered the last sentence with a breathy sigh.

With a shake of his head he refused a third mouthful, fearing he might throw up in front of this sex pot.

Madame Dupont finished the raw meat. He watched the movement of her lips and listened to the slight chewing noises that emanated from them. He looked at her slender neck as she swallowed. His eyes were drawn further down to the red 'V' of her dressing–gown.

"Pardon," she said. "I forget your breakfast. Tu as faim?"

"Oui, un peu." Lindsay hoped his French accent wasn't too clumsy.

She rose from the table and busied herself at the other end of the kitchen. Her red silk dressing-gown finished at the knee. The girls at school hid their legs under tights or trousers for most of the year. When they unveiled them in the summer, they were either pasty white or almost orange from too much fake tan. Madame Dupont's calves reflected the same olive smoothness of her face. Lindsay leant over the table to see her feet. She was wearing gold flip-flops and there was scarlet polish on her toe nails.

The smell of coffee began to fill the kitchen. This never happened at home. His mother opened the jar of instant, plonked a spoonful in a mug and scalded it with boiling water. Madame Dupont was making proper coffee. The aroma was intoxicating.

Lindsay felt like he'd stepped outside his real world of GCSEs and adolescent angst into a film set for a romance. Here he was, the handsome macho hero with a sexy woman willingly making breakfast for him. His whole nervous system was on red alert with the intensity of it. The slight undulations in the wooden surface of the kitchen table registered like mountains beneath his finger-tips. The slicing of bread sounded like the swipe of a guillotine blade. His head was swimming in the smell of coffee whilst the tang of blood was still fresh on his tongue. But best of all was the sight of the red-sheathed woman with her back to him. Beneath the thin material was a female, an attractive, older, experienced female, who was definitely interested in him. He wondered if the belt tied loosely around her waist might accidentally come undone.

"Coffee," she said and placed two bowls of milky brown liquid on the table. "And bread."

A bowl wasn't what he was expecting. He looked to Madame Dupont for a lead as to what to do with it.

"You can dip the bread."

Lindsay took a slice, buttered it and then dunked into the dish. A film of melted butter transferred to the surface of the coffee. He lifted the bread to his mouth and bit off the soggy light brown end. It felt like grown-up comfort food.

Madame Dupont was drinking from her bowl now. Lindsay followed suit. As he placed it back on the table he felt dribbles of the warm liquid run down his chin. He put out his tongue to catch them. Then Madame Dupont leaned over the table and dabbed at his face with a cloth napkin. He could smell her coffee-scented breath. She licked her own lips as she dabbed at his. Lindsay's mother had cleaned his face a thousand times but Madame Dupont made it an intimate, sensuous gesture instead of a brisk display of motherly concern.

Between them they finished the bread and drained their coffee bowls. He looked at the kitchen clock. The hands had sped round and it was nearly lunchtime. He wondered if his hostess would get dressed. The belt had slipped slightly and a little more of her olive skinned bosom was on display.

"Shall we go upstairs?" she asked.

Lindsay's heart thumped wildly and he felt as though he might fall over if he stood up and tried to walk.

"Soon Corinne will be home," she said and offered her hand.

Lindsay swallowed hard, took her hand and followed her upstairs.

Before he left home his uncle had warned him about frogs' legs and snails, his granddad had said something about a nation of garlic-eating onion sellers pedalling around the country and his mother had gone into a panic about how many pairs of underpants and socks he might need. But nobody had warned him that he would be presented with the opportunity to lose his virginity to the mother of his exchange partner.

This sexual initiation was a moment he'd craved but now that it was upon him he was beset with fears. How would he know what to do? What if he couldn't perform? Would she expect him to provide condoms – that was the one thing that his mother had not included in his suitcase.

They paused outside his box room and Madame Dupont pushed the door open for him. "You will want to get ready," she said.

What was that supposed to mean? He could spray on a bit more deodorant and clean his teeth but was there something else he should do – some secret ritual they'd omitted from those embarrassing lessons at school about human reproduction?

"Shall I have a shower?" he asked, trying to discreetly sniff his armpits.

Madame Dupont looked puzzled. "If you wish but she will be here in thirty minutes."

Speed was obviously of the essence. Trembling, Lindsay moved closer to his hostess. He embraced her, allowing his hand to linger over the silk-covered mound of her breast.

"Non!" She jumped away from him. "Non! Do not touch."

Madame Dupont tried to cover herself more fully with the red gown as she backed down the landing.

Lindsay was still shaking but now it was with confusion and humiliation. Somehow he had totally misinterpreted her signals. What did she think of him? Would she tell the school? Would he be branded a sex offender and be hounded by press and public for the rest of his life?

"Corinne is a half-day at school." Madame Dupont was almost in her own bedroom now and speaking very quickly. Her English had suddenly deteriorated. "You go with her friends. I dress and do shopping."

Then she disappeared, firmly closing her bedroom door.

That French woman spoke a different language in more ways than one. Lindsay wished to be magically transported home so that he could pretend nothing had ever happened. But already there were noises downstairs. Corinne had arrived back with her mates. He took a deep breath and hoped he didn't look as bad as he felt.

Half an hour later he was staring at a bland-looking burger and a cardboard container of fries. Everything was identical to his usual fast-food hangout back in England but now it seemed like nursery fare. Too much had happened in the space of that short morning and such immature food would never satisfy him again.

But he ate well – he didn't want to face his hostess over the evening dinner table.

Spreading the word

If you've enjoyed this book, please, please hire billboards next to the busiest motorways in the realm and scream your newly discovered devotion to Quintessentially Quirky Tales in huge lettering. People driving past will appreciate the change of scene and lorry drivers will enjoy having something to study while they wait for 36 hours in a queuing system.

Feel free to spread recommendations for this collection by word of mouth. Go on – speak to your family, friends and neighbours. It'll be worth it just to see the shock on their faces. And let's not forget leaving positive feedback on Amazon. One 5-star review can talk down even the most suicidal author teetering on the edge of an office ledge…

Don't miss the other fun titles in the series

Fiddle of the Sphinx and other Quintessentially Quirky Tales

Mysterious new advisors plot to fool a Pharaoh, Willy Wonka resorts to desperate measures to rescue his recession-hit chocolate factory and a failing writer exacts a chilling revenge on her dismissive publisher.

Available now

An Ugly Way to Go and other Quintessentially Quirky tales

Repulsive Barry plans to make himself handsome by facing a firing squad, bus driver Bert wakes from a coma to discover he can miraculously speak every language on the planet and a rampaging werewolf puts the wind up a hapless pirate crew.

Available now

Made in the USA
Charleston, SC
10 June 2016